Millie's
Change of Fortune

PATRINA McKENNA

Publisher: Patrina McKenna

patrina.mckenna@outlook.com

ISBN-13: 978-1-8381827-4-8

DEDICATION

For my family and friends

1

JUST ANOTHER SATURDAY NIGHT

It was Saturday night – and another ready meal for one. At twenty-seven years old, Millie was left on the shelf. Things hadn't been too bad until six weeks ago when her flatmate, Shelley, had moved out. Like all of her friends, Shelley was now in a relationship. That left Millie with two problems; no single friend to go to the pub with and twice as much to pay for rent. Despite her best efforts, suitable flatmates were few and far between.

The microwave pinged, and Millie opened the door before sliding the hot plastic tray onto a cold plate. She ripped off the film cover and pulled a fork out of the kitchen drawer before sitting on the sofa to eat her meal. The TV was tuned into the local News channel, and Millie sighed at the sight of happy families enjoying the glorious Easter weekend weather at the fair in the field behind her apartment. She could hear the sound of music and laughter through her kitchen window; the last thing she needed was for the frivolity to be broadcast straight into her living room.

The reporter edged closer to the camera, flashed a white smile then ran a hand through her short blonde hair. 'I probably shouldn't tell you this, but I came to the fair last year. While I was here, I paid a visit to Madame Wilhelmina, and everything she predicted came true!' The reporter waved her left hand in the air. 'I'm engaged!'

Millie snorted as she changed the TV channel. What a load of old tosh! A game show would be preferable entertainment for a Saturday night. Millie poured a glass of wine and put her feet up, but she couldn't relax. She needed to find a flatmate sooner rather than later. Social media hadn't produced any suitable candidates. An hour passed before Millie thought of another option; put an advertisement in the village shop window. Millie checked the time; it was seven o'clock. The shop closed at eight on Saturdays. Millie poured another glass of wine. She'd write an advertisement and take it to the shop tonight.

*

On leaving the shop, Millie began to head back to her apartment. An image of the reporter on the News, waving her left hand in the air, flashed through Millie's mind. She chuckled to herself. It wouldn't hurt to pay a visit to Madame Wilhelmina. Millie was intrigued to know what she would say. If nothing else, it would help another dull Saturday evening pass by.

Madame Wilhelmina's wooden hut had a sign outside:

MADAME WILHELMINA

Teller of Fortunes for over forty years

OPEN HOURS:

Evenings – 6.00-9.00 p.m. (adults only)

There was a sign in a small window on the door which read:

STAY OUT

Millie shuffled her feet as she weighed up whether this was a good idea, or not. The door to the hut opened and a woman stepped outside. Millie noticed the sign had been changed to:

COME IN

Millie took a deep breath as she walked up to the door, turned the handle, and stepped inside. She gasped at the sight of Madame Wilhelmina, who was shrouded in black. Through the thick veil, Millie could make out the lady was wearing a mask too. Madame Wilhelmina punched the air and shouted: 'YES!!!' She stood up while removing her veil and face covering. Millie's knees shook at the sight of her BOSS!

'Brett! What on earth are you doing here?'

Brett removed the rest of his outer clothing until he stood there in a white T-shirt and jeans. 'Granny said I'd only need to cover for her for a couple of hours. She was right! Here put this on and take a seat.'

Brett pushed the black clothing into Millie's arms and held out Madame Wilhelmina's chair. Millie's mouth fell open before she shook her head. 'You have to be kidding me. I can't impersonate a fortune teller.'

Brett winked, and Millie's heart leapt at the sight of his long black eyelashes almost touching his cheek. Why did her boss have to be so gorgeous? At six-foot-four-inches tall, with sleek black hair and piercing green eyes, Brett stood out from the crowd. Millie was sure at least four of the recruitment consultants at *Miller, Casey & Harbottle* were in love with him. 'Well, *I've* done it for the last two hours; surely you can manage one? I need a drink. I've been talking in a high voice; and I've strained my vocal chords.' Brett winked again, and Millie giggled.

'I've had two glasses of wine. You can't let me loose on your grandmother's business.'

Brett rubbed his hands together. 'Great! The next hour will fly by. I've watched you at work. Your imagination exceeds all others.'

'What do you mean?'

Brett rubbed at the stubble on his chin as his eyes twinkled. 'I saw you move Sadie's cream doughnut onto Susie's plate when she wasn't looking.'

Millie gasped. 'You saw that?'

'I certainly did. Nothing escapes me in the office. You sent Sadie to pick up an interviewee while you made the move.'

Millie blushed. 'Well, I prefer Susie to Sadie. Go on; you can fire me now.'

Brett stood with hands on hips, and Millie kept direct contact with his incredible green eyes. 'I'll let you off if you help my granny.'

Millie huffed. 'Well, I suppose I need to shroud myself in black for the next hour. What should I say to these people?'

Brett's eyes twinkled. 'Granny advised me to "tell them what they want to hear". Find out what they're longing for, then tell them it will happen.'

Millie frowned. 'I can't do that. It's fake.'

Brett waved as he exited the hut. 'Just do your best, and I'll have a glass of Pinot Grigio waiting for you in the King's Head at the end of your shift.' Millie was relieved he left the sign on the window to: STAY OUT. She dressed in the gloomy outfit then changed the sign to: COME IN.

2

FORTUNE TELLER IN TRAINING

Millie ran her hands over the crystal ball in front of her. Her stomach churned; this was such a ridiculous idea. What was she going to say to people? She didn't have too long to think as the door to the hut opened, and an elderly lady stepped inside. Millie gestured for her to sit down, then lowered her voice and spoke slowly, 'What do you want to know, my dear?'

The lady's piercing green eyes widened. 'I want to know why you're sitting in my seat and where my grandson's gone?'

Millie jumped out of her chair. 'I'm so sorry. You must be Madame Wilhelmina. You can have your job back straight away. I was only covering for Brett as a favour. He needed to pop out; he won't be long.'

Madame Wilhelmina tutted. 'Well, that's very kind of you to make excuses for my grandson, but I've just seen him in the pub with his mates. I knew he wouldn't last a whole shift.' Wilhelmina stood up and squinted as she peered through the small glass window in the door while turning the "COME IN" sign to "STAY OUT". 'There's quite a queue forming outside. Make sure you ask each person to turn the sign round when they enter and again when they leave; otherwise you'll be up and down like a yoyo.'

Millie raised her arms in the air. 'But you're back now. You can take over.'

Wilhelmina shook her head. 'I need to return to the salsa competition in the village hall. My husband and I are in the final. I'll go out the back door, so no one sees me.' Wilhelmina reached inside her diamante purse and took out a ten-pound note. 'Here, this is for your trouble. Don't spend it just yet – you'll know when to use it.' Wilhelmina turned the sign round before she scuttled past Millie to make a quick exit.

Millie sat back down and held onto the crystal ball as her first client entered. 'Please turn the sign on the door. We must not be disturbed. What do you want to know, my dear?'

The young woman blew her nose. 'My boyfriend's been having an affair. I found out tonight. What should I do? I can't leave him – I have nowhere to go.'

Millie stared at the red-faced woman. She looked presentable. Her light brown hair was tied back in a ponytail, and she clutched a Ted Baker handbag. 'What's your name, my dear? Do you have a job?'

The woman's bloodshot eyes widened. 'My name's Tanya, and I'm an Advertising Executive. This is sounding like an interview – I'm only here to find out where my future lies.'

Millie bowed her shrouded head until it was touching the crystal ball. She then sat upright. 'There is a safe haven waiting for you. You will find details in the window of the village shop. Do not delay. Your new life is just around the corner. Everything happens for a reason.'

Tanya held a hand to her chest. 'Thank you so much. You've been a great help.'

Four clients later, Millie was enjoying herself. Things were going well until Jordan from the office strode into the hut. Was this a joke? Millie swallowed hard before speaking, 'Please turn the sign on the door. We must not be disturbed. What do you want to know, my dear?'

Jordan sat down before running his fingers through his tousled blonde hair. He lowered his grey eyes before speaking, 'There's this girl I like where I work. I don't have the guts to ask her out. I want to know if she features in my future.'

Millie sighed. She knew that top-performing recruitment consultant, Jordan, had a thing for high-flying senior recruitment consultant Sadie. She was surprised he was so vulnerable; he was always loud and confident in the office. This would be an easy one to sort out. Millie touched her forehead to the crystal ball. 'I can see you both in your office. Her name begins with "S". She's just won an award, and you are captivated by her beauty. Long red hair, long legs, large shiny green eyes – your true love is such a stunner.' Millie sat upright. It was a shame that Sadie wasn't beautiful on the inside too. How could she stop Jordan from making a big mistake?

Millie placed her forehead on the crystal ball again. 'It's not good news, I'm afraid. Your true love admires someone else. He's very tall with green eyes and black hair. He has a better job than you. You need to lower your expectations.'

Jordan sat back in his chair. 'Wow! I think you should get a refund on that crystal ball; it's not tuned in right. I knew this was a mistake, but Brett insisted I had my fortune told. I would never have come here if he wasn't the boss. At least when I get back to the pub, I can tell him Sadie's got the hots for him.' Jordan stood up. 'You couldn't be further from the truth about the girl I like, her name begins with "M", and she looks nothing like Sadie.'

Millie's heart raced. 'Please turn the sign on the door before you leave.'

After two more customers, Millie glanced at the time on her phone. It was nine o'clock. She turned the sign on the door before pulling off the black clothing and reaching into her bag for a hairbrush. Could she be the love of Jordan's life? She'd never considered him an option before. The recruitment consultants looked down on the administrators – or so she thought.

Looking in a mirror, Millie saw an attractive twenty-seven-year-old woman looking back. The sand-coloured eyeshadow she'd put on this morning enhanced her cornflower blue eyes, and the hair mask she'd worn for an hour last night had brought a sheen to her long wavy black hair. A pale blue T-shirt and grey jeans wouldn't have been her first choice to wear for a drink in the pub with a potential admirer, but Millie couldn't complain. Over the last hour, things had taken a turn for the better.

As Millie stepped inside the pub, her phone rang. She saw Brett waving to her, and she waved back before pointing to her phone and going outside. 'Hello, Millie speaking.'

'Oh, hi, Millie. My name's Tanya, and I've just seen your advertisement for a flatmate. Is there any chance we could meet up tonight? You see, I've just found out my boyfriend's having an affair and I don't want to spend another night at his place. I'd rather leave before he gets home.'

Millie sighed; it would have been better if Tanya had waited until tomorrow to contact her. Still, she felt sorry for the poor girl. 'Of course, that's no problem. I'm in the King's Head. We can get to know one another over a drink; some of my work colleagues are here too. See you soon.'

Tanya breathed a sigh of relief. 'Wait! Before you go, you won't know who I am. I'll be carrying a mint green Ted Baker handbag, so you'll easily spot me.'

Millie smiled to herself. 'I'll look out for you. I'm wearing a blue T-shirt and grey jeans, and I'll be drinking a Pinot Grigio.'

Tanya giggled. 'Buy a bottle; it's my favourite. I'll pay you when I get there. You're a lifesaver! See you soon.'

3

A MISUNDERSTANDING

Brett was keen to take Millie to one side. 'What have you been saying to Jordan?'

Millie chuckled. 'I insinuated that Sadie found you attractive rather than him. As you know, Sadie isn't my favourite person, and it would be cruel to push Jordan into her clutches.'

Brett's mouth fell open. 'But you don't mind sacrificing me?'

Millie was surprised at Brett's comment. She'd expected to be reprimanded for speaking badly about one of their star players – Brett's guard was obviously down after a few beers. Millie sipped the Pinot Grigio he'd bought her and signalled to the bar person for a bottle and another glass.

Brett frowned. 'I don't think you should drink a whole bottle. You said you'd had two glasses before you came out tonight. I wouldn't want you making a fool of yourself.'

Millie huffed. 'I think I've already made a fool of myself – impersonating your grandmother. Anyway, I have a friend coming, and I'm sure she'll drink most of it.'

Brett relaxed his shoulders. 'That's good then. Thanks for helping me out and for not letting on to Jordan that my granny's an eccentric old bat.'

Millie raised her eyebrows. 'Your grandmother's lovely.'

Brett's mouth fell open. 'You've met her?'

'I sure have. She came into the hut to check on you. She wasn't surprised you didn't stay around for a whole shift.'

Brett's eyes twinkled. 'Granny knows what I'm like. I'd love to have seen your reaction when Jordan turned up. Did he divulge any intimate secrets? You can tell me; I'm the boss.'

Millie lowered her eyes. 'He said something about a girl in the office whose name begins with "M". It sounds like he's quite taken with her.'

Brett rubbed his chin. 'Oh, that'll be Mandy … no wait … Melanie – she's more his type.'

Millie's heart sank as the door to the pub opened, and Tanya wandered in. Millie waved to her before turning to pour her a glass of wine. How could she have been so stupid to think Jordan would be attracted to her? Millie held out the glass. 'Hello, Tanya, I'm Millie, and this is my boss, Brett.'

Brett took hold of Tanya's hand and kissed it. Millie cringed, the poor girl had just broken up with her boyfriend, and now she was being hit on by the most attractive man in the pub. Tanya lifted her hand and slapped Brett's face. She grabbed Millie's arm and guided her to a small table in the corner of the room. 'What's the chance of that – your boss being my ex?'

Millie glanced at Brett, who was rubbing his cheek with one hand and scratching his head with the other. 'Does Brett know you've broken up with him?'

'Not yet; I've left him a note.'

'How did you find out he's having an affair?'

'Because a photo of a red-head flashed up on his phone just before he left to go out tonight. He said he was going to see his grandmother. I can't believe he lied to me!'

Millie's jaw dropped as the pub door opened, and

Sadie strutted in. She headed straight for Brett. 'Brett! I tried to call you earlier. I couldn't get hold of you, so I spoke to Jordan, who invited me here for a drink. I wanted to tell you the news about the *Picard Ratcliffe* vacancy – I've filled it! They're so pleased with me that I need to pop over to Paris on Tuesday to discuss a restructuring they're planning in France.'

Tanya jumped up. 'I need to get home to rip up that note.'

Millie raised her eyebrows. 'What about the slap on the cheek?'

'I'll go over and apologise. I'll say it was a misunderstanding.'

Millie watched a bemused Brett wave to Tanya as she left the pub swinging her Ted Baker bag. Millie grabbed her glass and the bottle of wine. She avoided Brett and Sadie by sitting next to Jordan. She placed the bottle on the table. 'If you get another glass, you can help me drink this. I've just had the worst evening possible.'

Jordan didn't question Millie as he walked up to the bar to request a glass. He returned and topped her glass up before filling his. 'Would you like to talk about it?'

'Not really. Unless you know of someone who

would be my perfect flatmate, I'll need to start living in my car soon if I don't find one.'

Jordan smiled. 'Would I be acceptable?'

'You?! You have your own house.'

'Well, I do, until the end of next week. The one I'm moving into needs renovating. I was thinking of booking into a hotel for a while, but that would be quite lonely *and* expensive. What do you think? Shall we live together?'

Millie's cheeks flared up. 'What about moving in with Mandy or Melanie? They may have spare rooms.'

Jordan's grey eyes twinkled. 'They're not my type. I promise I'll behave. I'll load the dishwasher, do my own washing, and make the occasional meal for two if you're around.' Jordan frowned. 'You do have a dishwasher, don't you?'

Millie nodded. 'Of course.'

'I think we should seal the deal then.' Jordan held out his glass, and Millie clinked hers against it.

Brett turned to speak to Millie, 'How do you know Tanya?'

Millie's head was spinning. 'Oh, I bumped into her earlier. We only met today.'

Brett rubbed his cheek again before turning to face the pub door, which had opened to a roar of cheers and round of applause. Wilhelmina held a gold trophy in the air. She waved to Brett. 'We did it! Your grandfather and I won first prize. I've just popped in to let everyone know. Grandpa is struggling to get out of the car with all that hip wiggling. We're heading off home for an early night.'

Wilhelmina rummaged through a carrier bag. 'Oh, before I forget. Here's a book of raffle tickets. They cost ten pounds a strip. One of the members of the Over 60's Club is raffling off the use of their holiday home on the English Riviera for the summer.' Wilhelmina glared at Brett. 'We do get some eccentric old bats at the club. More money than they know what to do with. Make sure you buy some tickets before they get snapped up.'

Jordan and Sadie stared at Brett. Sadie's face dropped. 'That's your grandmother?'

Brett held his shoulders back. 'It certainly is.'

Millie grabbed her purse and pushed past Jordan. 'Excuse me. I need to buy a strip of tickets before they all go. Would you like me to get you some too? Jordan took out his wallet and handed Millie a ten-pound note. 'That would be great, thanks, flatmate.'

Sadie's head spun round. 'Flatmate? What do you

mean by that?'

'I'm moving in with Millie while my new home is being renovated.'

Brett looked over at Millie and then back to Jordan. Suddenly the letter "M" took on a whole new meaning.

Millie returned with the tickets, and she held out a strip for Jordan. He shook his head. 'Don't give them to me; I'll lose them. I'd rather leave them in your safe hands.' Millie folded the tickets and put them in her purse.

Brett took out his phone and sent a text:

Granny, is my current girlfriend the right one?

Brett's phone buzzed with an answer:

No, dear.

Brett's cheek still smarted. He couldn't forgive Tanya for humiliating him like that in the pub. She also didn't have his grandmother's approval. Brett had no alternative but to break up with her in the morning.

4

RETURN TO THE OFFICE

On Tuesday morning, Brett called a team meeting. Fifteen members of *Miller, Casey & Harbottle* entered the boardroom, coffees in hand. Brett sat at the head of the table. 'It's great to see you all after the Easter break. We only have one person absent today, and that's Sadie, who's in Paris.' There were a few raised eyebrows, and Brett continued, 'Sadie advised me on Saturday night that she's filled the *Picard Ratcliffe* vacancy and has now been invited to work with the management team on their restructuring in France. Excellent work by Sadie to secure more lucrative business.'

There was a polite round of applause in Sadie's absence, and Melanie whispered to Susie, 'Raff Picard flew her over in his private jet. Brett would be livid if he knew she was staying in Raff's Paris apartment and that she's planning to string her "day trip" out for the week. I'm sure *Picard Ratcliffe* are trying to poach her; we'll lose a shed-load of business if she goes to work for them.'

'Why would she want to work for a dog food brand?'

'They're not just any dog food brand – they're the market leaders. I buy their Mushy Meat Mocktails for little Lucy as a treat on special occasions.'

'Yuck! They sound horrible. Your poor Chihuahua.'

Melanie could feel Brett's eyes boring into the side of her head. She was on a final warning for whispering in meetings. She turned around and smiled sweetly. 'That's brilliant news about Sadie.'

Brett frowned. 'Is there any other news I need to be made aware of that happened over the weekend?'

Susie held her hand up. 'I went to see Madame Wilhelmina at the fairground, and she said something interesting.'

Brett locked eyes with Millie, and the connection between the two of them didn't go unnoticed by the rest of the team. Brett rubbed his chin. 'What did Madame Wilhelmina say? Of course, everyone knows to take fortune telling with a pinch of salt.' Brett chuckled to hide his embarrassment.

Susie's cheeks were flushed as she spoke, 'She said there was going to be a major shake-up where I work.'

A tingle ran down Brett's spine. 'Did you tell her *where* you worked?'

'No. Her words have been bothering me ever since.'

Brett narrowed his eyes at Millie, and she shrugged her shoulders. Again, another intimate connection between the two that sent knowing looks around the room. Brett struggled to hide his irritation. 'Well, if that's all we have to share, then I suggest we get back to work.'

Jordan raised his hand before speaking, 'There is some other news; I'm moving in with Millie.' That revelation called for gasps all round.

Susie and Melanie watched Millie and Brett whispering at the drinks machine. What on earth was going on? From being the office wallflower, Millie had now gained the attention of both Brett and Jordan.

Brett kept his back to the room as he locked eyes with Millie. 'So Susie didn't turn up on your shift in the hut?'

Millie shook her head. 'Your grandmother must have given her the news.'

'My granny is trying to stir things up. She must have recognised Susie from a brochure or on our website. I'm sure she spies on me.'

'Why would your grandmother want to stir things up?'

'Because, in her eyes, I'm an under-achiever. My two brothers are the golden boys.'

Millie's eyes widened. 'How can you be an "under-achiever"? You manage this business.'

Brett sighed. 'I'm not settled down. That's what's bothering her.'

'What do your brothers do?'

'Chad's an artist, and Danny lives the life of Riley as the self-appointed manager of my grandparents' affairs. Trust me; they don't need anyone managing their affairs – they're not senile yet.'

Millie rubbed her forehead, and Melanie whispered to Susie, 'I think they may be having a lovers' tiff.'

Millie composed herself. 'I can't see how they're the golden boys. You've worked your guts off to get this far. Why can't Chad and Danny settle down? Where do they live?'

'Danny lives in my grandparents' place in Devon.

Chad lives across the road from him in a beach hut. At least Chad pays for his accommodation; I have some respect for him. As far as settling down is concerned, they're a long way off from that. They're much younger than me. I'm thirty-eight, and they're in their late twenties. So as far as my granny's concerned, I'm the one destined to lose my bachelorhood first. I'm sure she just wants a wedding to go to so she can wear a hat.'

Millie sniggered. 'Can't you take her to the races? She can wear a hat if you go on Ladies Day.'

It was now Brett's turn to chuckle. 'You may have a point there!'

Melanie nudged Susie. 'They're laughing. It looks like they've made up. Whoever would have guessed that Brett would have eyes for Millie?'

Susie looked over at Jordan, who was watching his boss chatting to the previously quiet and unassuming administrator, and she nudged Melanie. 'Don't forget that Jordan's moving in with Millie. How did that come about?'

Jordan stood up and headed for the drinks machine. He placed a protective hand on Millie's shoulder. 'Sorry to interrupt you two, but I need to book a date with Millie to discuss my imminent arrival at her humble abode.'

Brett playfully punched Jordan's arm. 'Less of the "humble". I'm sure Millie's apartment is very homely.'

Millie blushed. 'Humble is the right word, I'm afraid. I'm sure you'd have been more comfortable living in your new home with the renovation work going on.'

Melanie's eyes widened. 'They're fighting over her now. We'll have to find out what changed over the weekend. She may have bought a new perfume. If so, I want one.'

Susie giggled. 'I would, too, if I wasn't happily married.'

Brett's phone vibrated, and he read the text:

> *Winner of the raffle to be announced at 7.00 tonight in the King's Head. Pass the message on. Love Grandma x*

Brett glanced at Millie, then Jordan. 'Why don't we all go to the pub tonight? You two can have your "date", and I'll tag along as I'm a lonely old bachelor now I've thrown Tanya out.'

Millie gulped. 'You finished with her?'

Brett headed towards his office. 'I certainly did. My granny didn't approve. Do you see what I'm up against? My private life is harder to manage than this business. Talking of that, I'll see you in my office in ten, Jordan. We need to discuss the *Ennis Everglades* contract; they've threatened to pull the plug if we don't source at least four candidates by Friday. I'll need you to cover for Sadie this week. Don't be surprised if she stays in Paris with Raff for a spot of sightseeing.'

Brett winked at Millie, and Melanie swooned. 'Did you see that? He winked at her. Madame Wilhelmina was spot on. There's been a massive shake-up at the office already.'

5

RAFFLE WINNER

Millie munched on a cheeseburger. She wiped her mouth before speaking, 'Are you sure you won't let me pay for mine?'

Jordan stabbed at his chips. 'It's the least I can do. You helped me out of a hole this afternoon by searching for candidates for *Ennis Everglades*. You were great on the phone, by the way. You should get Brett to pay for formal training. You'll be snapping at Sadie's heels within a year.'

Millie blushed. 'Melanie thinks that *Picard Ratcliffe* will try to poach Sadie. Do you think they'd move to an in-house solution rather than work with us?'

Jordan placed his fork down. 'Now, there's a

thought. They certainly have enough business to set up their own recruitment team. That's always a risk when we deal with large organisations. Still, many companies would rather outsource than do our jobs.' Jordan picked up his steak baguette and frowned. 'The *Picard Ratcliffe* contract is huge. If we lose it, Brett will need to make some changes in the office.'

Millie's eyes widened. 'Surely, Sadie has a clause in her employment contract to stop her from jumping ship to one of our clients?'

Jordan shrugged his shoulders. 'Brett's not that great with HR; it's his weakness. I don't have a clause in my contract to stop me from doing anything.'

Millie winced. 'Do you think we should give Brett the "heads up"? He should know if we have some HR loopholes.'

Jordan shook his head. 'I'd rather not. We'll have less freedom if our employment contracts are tightened up. As things are now, any of us can leave and go to any business we wish, and we only need to give a month's notice. That includes competitors, customers, or even setting up on our own.' Jordan held a finger to his lips and nodded towards the door. 'Shush, Brett's coming. Let's keep this between ourselves.'

Brett opened his wallet and took out two strips of raffle tickets before handing them to Millie. 'Here –

they're going to announce the raffle winner at seven o'clock, and I need to pop back to the office to interview a candidate as a favour for Sadie.' Brett smiled as he headed out of the pub. 'If I win, I'll buy a bottle of champagne to celebrate. Don't get your hopes up too much, though; I never win anything.'

Millie reached for her purse and took out their raffle tickets. She glanced at the numbers; should she have the first strip or the second? She decided she should have numbers one to five and Jordan should have six to ten. If Jordan had gone to the bar to buy his own tickets, he wouldn't have got there before her. Millie handed Jordan his strip and placed hers on the table next to her wine glass.

At seven o'clock, Madame Wilhelmina entered the pub carrying a bucket of folded-up raffle tickets and an envelope. The bar person rang a bell, and Wilhelmina glanced around the room before rummaging around in the bucket and pulling out a ticket. There was an air of anticipation as Wilhelmina paused to confirm there was only one esteemed prize this evening – the use of a holiday home on the English Riviera for the summer.

The suspense amongst the regulars in the pub was palpable. Previous raffle prizes in the King's Head had consisted of boxes of biscuits, unwanted cuddly toys, and the occasional bottle of wine. Wilhelmina unravelled the ticket and waved it in the air for all to see. 'The winner is Number Three.'

Millie waved her strip of tickets in the air. 'It's me! That's my ticket!'

Wilhelmina walked over and handed Millie the envelope. 'Here are the details of your prize, my dear. May you have a fun-filled summer.'

Millie was lost for words as Wilhelmina made her exit. Jordan punched the air. 'You did it! You won. Open the envelope so we can see where exactly this holiday home is.'

Millie's hands were shaking. 'I feel bad about this, Jordan. The ticket may have been yours. I bought both strips at the same time.'

Jordan grabbed Millie's hand. 'Don't be silly. Logically, the first set of numbers should be yours; you were up at the bar first to buy the tickets. I've never seen anyone move so fast. Besides, what would I do with a holiday home? Brett moans when I take a week off, let alone a whole summer. That's a point; he's good on the HR side when it comes to holidays; we're all limited to a measly four weeks.'

Millie's hand flew to her mouth. 'I've taken two weeks already this year. I'll have hardly any time to spend on the English Riviera.'

Jordan sighed; he could see Millie's predicament. 'Why don't you open the envelope, and we'll try to find a solution.'

Millie ripped the envelope open and pulled out a card:

WELCOME TO THE ENGLISH RIVIERA

Arrival: 2.00 p.m. on 1st June

Departure: 2.00 p.m. on 31st August

Address: Harbottle Penthouse, Devon

Terms & Conditions: Your job at *Miller, Casey & Harbottle* will be kept open for you during your summer sabbatical.

Millie's mouth fell open, and she handed the card to Jordan, who burst out laughing. 'This is some sort of a joke!'

The pub door flew open, and Brett breezed in. He smiled at Jordan. 'What's so funny?'

Jordan handed the card to Brett. 'You need to sit down before you read this. Millie won the raffle, and here is her prize.'

Brett read the card, then flopped back in his chair. 'What is she playing at now?'

Millie raised her eyebrows. 'I'm not playing at anything.'

Brett sighed. 'Not you. My granny – the eccentric Madame Wilhelmina. The penthouse is my grandparents' holiday home; it comes with its very own squatter – my brother, Danny.'

Millie gulped. 'Your brother will be there too?'

'Of course, I told you he lives there for free while he "manages" my grandparents' affairs.'

Millie was taken back to their conversation at the coffee machine in the office. 'And your other brother, Chad, lives over the road in a beach hut.'

'Well remembered.'

Jordan scratched his head as he stared at Brett. 'Your grandmother is Madame Wilhelmina? You didn't tell me that when you sent me to see her. That was pretty cruel of you, mate; I may have shared a secret with her.'

Millie blushed and decided to keep quiet. Brett's thoughts were elsewhere. 'Now I've got a huge problem at the office – how will we cope without Millie for three months?'

Millie continued to blush. 'You needn't worry, I only have two weeks holiday left this year.'

Brett read the card again. 'My granny's arranged for you to take a sabbatical. This means we'll keep your job open while you're away. I'll need to hire a temp.'

Jordan raised his eyebrows. 'Can your

grandmother do that?'

Brett shifted in his seat. 'Wilhelmina Harbottle's a silent partner in the business – although it appears she doesn't know the meaning of the word "silent".'

Millie's head was spinning. 'What if I turn the prize down? I can't afford to take three months off. I'll still need to pay the rent on my apartment.'

Brett had a solution. 'Jordan will pay the rent; it's the least he can do while he's staying at yours.'

Millie stared at Jordan. 'I didn't think you'd need to stay with me for the whole summer. Won't your renovation work be completed sooner than that?'

Brett kicked Jordan under the table, and he winced before answering, 'Oh, I'll definitely need to stay at yours until at least September. Brett's right – I'll cover the rent.'

6

MISS POPULAR

Jordan entered Brett's office and closed the door behind him. 'What was that all about last night? Why have you set me up to pay Millie's rent for the summer?'

Brett placed his pen on his desk and sat back in his chair. 'Take a seat, Jordan.' Jordan did as requested, and Brett continued, 'You don't need to worry about Millie's rent. I'll pay it while she's on secondment to my grandparents' holiday home.'

Jordan frowned. 'On secondment?'

Brett lowered his eyes. 'I can't think of any other way to describe it. My granny's up to something, and I can't work out what. All I would ask is that we keep this between the two of us. I wouldn't want Millie to know I have my suspicions.'

Jordan's eyes were on stalks. 'Why can't you just

stand up to your grandmother?'

Brett shrugged his shoulders. 'Because she's always right.'

*

It was lunchtime before the steady stream of people entering Brett's office subsided, and Millie got the chance to knock on his door.

'Come in.'

Millie entered and closed the door. She stood with her back against it. 'I have given your grandmother's raffle prize serious consideration and have decided to turn it down. The whole thing has been a fix. She even paid for my tickets. I'm very uncomfortable, and your grandmother should be worried she'll be sued for obtaining money illegally – or whatever the terminology is. I saw at least ten people buy raffle tickets on Saturday night.' Realisation then hit Millie, and she pointed at Brett. 'You should be annoyed more than most; you bought two strips! Your grandmother conned you out of twenty pounds!'

Brett tried not to smile as Millie folded her arms and stamped her foot. He thought she looked cute when she frowned. Brett reached inside the top drawer of his desk and took out his wallet and phone before standing up and grabbing his jacket off the coat stand behind the door. He stood in front of Millie. 'Well, will you let me out of my office to buy some lunch, or not?'

Millie stood firm. 'Not until you listen to me.'

Brett sighed. 'Well, you'll have to come to lunch with me then. I can't concentrate on an empty stomach.'

Melanie rushed to the office window before gesturing for Susie to join her. 'Quick! She's getting in his car.'

Susie put down her salad box and ran to the window. 'Lucky Millie!'

Jordan ended a call and then glanced over to see what the commotion was about. 'What's going on?'

Melanie shook her head. 'Nothing.'

Jordan frowned. Those two were always up to no good. Brett was right; what would they do without Millie for three months? It was surprising, but he'd never really noticed Millie before. Jordan had to admit that when Sadie was in the office, he couldn't take his eyes off *her*. It was a shock when Madame Wilhelmina had guessed who he had a crush on. Thankfully he'd put her off the scent by saying her name began with "M". Wait a minute! Now that Jordan knew Madame Wilhelmina was Brett's grandmother, her prediction took on a whole new meaning:

> *'It's not good news, I'm afraid. Your true love admires someone else. He's very tall with green eyes and black hair. He has a better job than you. You need to lower your expectations.'*

Madame Wilhelmina was trying to get her grandson married off to Sadie! After an initial stab of annoyance, Jordan didn't mind at all. He'd been concerned that Brett was becoming close to the beautiful raven-haired, blue-eyed administrator who'd been under everyone's radar until a few days ago. After Jordan's discussion with Brett this morning, he was under no illusion his boss did whatever his grandmother wanted. That paved the way for Jordan with Millie. He rubbed his hands together and went to look for Brett; the least he could do was offer to buy him lunch. It was kind of Brett to secretly pay for Millie's rent for three months.

Brett's office door was shut, and there was no one inside. Jordan called to Melanie, 'Any idea where Brett's gone?'

Melanie sat up straight and waited to see the expression on Jordan's face when she answered him, 'He's taken Millie out for lunch.'

It was worth taking in every detail when Jordan's face dropped, and he ran a hand through his tousled blonde hair. His grey eyes clouded over too. It was evident Jordan had moved on from Sadie and now had the hots for his new flatmate, Millie. Melanie glanced over at Susie, who winked back at her.

*

In the coffee shop, Brett listened to Millie's reasonings and excuses while he ate his cheese and ham baguette.

He let her words wash over him as he constructed a counterattack that would stop Millie in her tracks and send her off to the English Riviera.

Millie's coffee had gone cold, and her chicken salad sandwich remained untouched. She sat back in her chair. 'So, there you are. There's no way I'll be spending the whole summer at the seaside. You won't need to find a temp to replace me as I'm not going anywhere.'

Brett pushed his plate to one side. His piercing green eyes locked with Millie's, and her stomach churned. He was serious as he spoke, 'The subject's not open for debate. I've already appointed a temp, who'll be starting next week. That will give you time for a hand-over period. You won the raffle and must abide by the terms and conditions of entering the draw.'

Millie tried to speak, and Brett held a finger to his lips. 'As your boss and grandson of the raffle organiser, I have a responsibility for your welfare. I'll drive you to Devon on your first day to ensure you get there on time. There's no way out, Millie. Just relax and enjoy the summer.'

Millie sipped her cold coffee; she couldn't eat anything. Brett turned to look at a message on his phone, and she slipped the sandwich into her bag. Her phone vibrated, and she read a message from Jordan:

Are you available at 7.00 tonight for a takeaway at yours? If so, I'll bring it with me. Chinese or Indian? You can show me how the dishwasher works before I move in on Friday. We can catch up after lunch in the office. See you soon. Jordan

7

MOVING DAY

Friday had arrived, and Jordan threw an arm around Millie. 'There was no need for you to take the day off too. Although I'm glad you did. I'd offer you a coffee, but everything's packed. The removal team have been here since the crack of dawn. When we get to my new place, I'll do my best to find the kettle.'

Millie pulled a flask out of her bag. 'There's no need to rush. I bought coffee with me and sandwiches. I wasn't sure what state your new place would be in with all the renovation work you're planning. You must be so excited you're getting the keys today.'

Jordan nodded. 'I certainly am! It's taken months to get here. I'll never move again.'

Millie smiled. 'Ah, I see. So you're moving into

your "forever home".'

Jordan frowned. 'I hadn't thought of it like that. I hope my future wife likes it.' Jordan turned to face Millie. 'Will you give me your honest opinion on it when we get there? I've had no one to challenge my thought process before. It doesn't look much now, but I can see how it will be great.'

Millie felt quite excited about the prospect. 'What if I don't like it?'

Jordan's face dropped. 'Then it may not be my "forever home". I'll have to find somewhere else and put the unfortunate experience down to my bad taste and rash decision-making.'

*

Two hours later, Jordan pressed a remote control to open the electric gates of his new home. He steered his Porsche down the long winding gravel drive and parked outside a large, imposing three-story building with gabled roofs, towers, and turrets. Millie gasped and Jordan explained, 'It's Victorian, and I fell in love with what she once was – and what she could be again. She needs a lot of work.'

Jordan climbed out of the car and opened Millie's door. She stepped onto the gravel drive and took in the sight of the dilapidated building and overgrown gardens. 'I love it!'

'You do?'

'Yes. I've always wanted to live somewhere like this.'

'Isn't it a bit soon? We're not in a relationship yet.'

Millie punched Jordan's arm. 'I didn't mean in *this* house, and I didn't mean with you!'

Jordan feigned disappointment, and Millie linked her arm through his. 'Come on! I can't wait to have a look inside.'

The couple climbed the wooden steps onto the porch with intricately carved wooden spindles and weather-beaten handrails, and Millie turned around to admire the view. 'It would be lovely sitting out here on a summer's evening. You should get one of those two-seater garden swings with a trellis. That way, you could train a climbing rose over it. It would smell wonderful.'

Jordan reached for his phone and brought up an image. 'One like this?'

Millie looked at his phone. 'That's exactly what I meant.'

Jordan grinned. 'I have one on order.'

Millie gasped before being swept off her feet. 'What are you doing?!'

'Carrying you over the threshold.'

'What?!!'

'You seem like marriage material to me. We have

the same taste in everything.'

Jordan placed Millie's feet on the ground, and she burst out laughing. 'You are so annoying. I'm beginning to regret letting you stay at my place for the summer.'

Jordan winked at her. 'Don't forget you'll be on the English Riviera – I'll just have to be annoying from afar.' Jordan frowned. 'What will you be doing for twelve weeks? It'll get boring just lounging around.'

Millie sighed. 'Exactly. I've tried to tell Brett, but he's insisting I go ahead with his grandmother's plan. If he weren't the boss, I wouldn't be going. Anyway, less talk of my raffle prize. I want to know what you have planned for this amazing place. Are you going to show me around?'

*

It was eight o'clock before Millie and Jordan entered the King's Head in need of sustenance – Millie's sandwiches and cakes had been devoured by lunchtime. They weren't surprised to see Brett sitting at one of the tables, but they were surprised he was sitting in a huddle with Melanie and Susie. The small group were balancing laptops on the table and taking care not to spill their drinks.

Jordan raised his eyebrows at Millie before guiding her to their colleagues' table. 'Is this a private party, or can anyone join in?'

Brett's head jerked around. 'Jordan! Oh, hi Millie, you're here too. Grab a couple of drinks and come and join us.'

Millie whispered to Jordan, 'I need food.'

Jordan stood behind Brett. 'You all look busy. Have you eaten?'

Brett shook his head. 'We've had a disastrous day at the office. There's no time to eat.'

Millie gulped, and Jordan squeezed her arm. 'Well, we'll be of no use to you if we don't eat. How about I order pizzas all round?'

Melanie and Susie looked up from their laptops and managed weak smiles at Jordan, who took that as a signal they were as hungry as he was. 'I'll place the food order and get Millie a drink, then you can tell us what's going on.'

With Millie and Jordan seated at the table, Brett sank back in his chair. 'Sadie's resigned. She's left already. She's only on four weeks' notice and has decided to forsake her final month's salary to stay in France and set up an in-house recruitment team for *Picard Ratcliffe*.'

Millie choked on her wine, and Jordan slapped her back before locking eyes with her in an all-knowing glance. Brett continued, 'I've reached out to an employment lawyer, and we're seriously lacking on the HR front. I need to issue everyone with new contracts without delay. There are far too many loopholes in our current ones. Even *I* could leave at the drop of a hat.'

Susie held up a shaking hand, and Brett stared at her. 'Don't forget what Madame Wilhelmina told me at the fair – I think her exact words were: "There's going to be a major shake-up at the place where you work".'

Brett shivered, and Millie grabbed Jordan's knee. He placed his hand over hers and squeezed it. Melanie noticed the move and nudged Susie before narrowing her eyes at Millie. What was their friend playing at? She'd had lunch with Brett on Wednesday, and, just two days later, she was flirting with Jordan.

Millie removed her hand and combed her fingers through her shiny black hair; her cornflower blue eyes were sparkling. She was pleased that Brett was tightening up the contracts. She hadn't agreed with Jordan that they shouldn't tell him. She was also delighted that Sadie had left the business.

Jordan was frowning as he spoke to Brett, 'What does this mean, Brett? What's the bottom line? How many employees will we need to lose?'

Millie gulped, and Susie and Melanie lowered their eyes while they waited for a drained Brett to answer, 'I don't know for sure yet, but there will need to be significant cutbacks. There's also a chance our key players won't sign their new contracts and an even bigger chance that Sadie will poach them to join her team. We may not have a business by the end of the summer.'

Jordan flopped back in his chair, and Millie's heart sank. There was, however, one positive out of all of this. There was no way Brett would let her take the summer off now; he'd need her in the office.

8

WELCOME TO THE ENGLISH RIVIERA

Jordan opened the door of Millie's apartment for Brett to enter. 'Are you sure you've got time to drive Millie down to Devon? I could take the day off and drive her there myself. Surely, you'd be of more use meeting with *Ennis Everglades* today. You said we needed to pull out the "big guns" for our major clients.'

Brett placed an arm around Jordan's shoulders. 'You are a "big gun". You're my second in command now that Sadie's gone. I couldn't have managed without you over the last month. By the way, your new contract will be ready for you to sign next week. Don't go doing anything stupid before I've got you locked in. I'll need to lose a few more employees, but you're not one of them.'

Millie walked into the living room, wheeling her

case, and Brett stepped forward to take it from her. 'I'll put this in the car. See you outside.'

Millie reached up to kiss Jordan's cheek. 'You heard what Brett said: "Don't go doing anything stupid." That covers forgetting to put a tablet in the dishwasher; washing red socks with white shirts; using my hairdryer – I'm not taking it. There's one in the penthouse.'

Jordan looked forlorn, and Millie held his shoulders. 'What's wrong?'

'I won't be signing a new contract?'

'What?!'

'I can't be tied down to a six months' notice period. I have plans.'

'What plans?'

Jordan kissed Millie's cheek. 'That secret's between us. Off you go now, don't keep Brett waiting. Enjoy the summer!'

Brett was standing outside his top-of-the-range Mercedes. He opened the door for Millie, who turned to face him. 'Are you sure you can do without me with everything that's going on at work?'

Brett's handsome face froze. 'Of course, the temp is great. Thanks for training him up.'

Millie frowned. 'I *will* have a job to return to in September, won't I?'

Brett gave a lopsided grin. 'You'll deserve a job after helping my granny out for three months. If the business is still afloat, there'll always be a place for you. I'm just lucky I have Jordan. He'll help me out of this mess.'

Brett turned on the engine and sped down the road. Millie clung to her seat. 'What will your grandmother want me to do?'

Brett turned to glance at his passenger. 'I have absolutely no idea.'

*

Four hours later, Millie stepped out of Brett's car and set foot in Devon. She breathed in the sea air before turning to her boss. 'I'm nervous. Which property has a penthouse?'

Brett pointed to a hotel. 'That one.'

'The penthouse is part of a hotel?!'

'My grandparents own the hotel.'

Millie threw her hand to her mouth. 'What?!!'

'If nothing else, you'll have a great sea view.'

'Will I get bored?'

'Not if my granny has anything to do with it.'

Brett dragged Millie's case through the hotel foyer and smiled at the attentive staff who recognised him. He strode to the lift and pressed the button for the Penthouse Suite. Millie nudged him and whispered, 'I thought it was your grandparents' holiday home. This isn't a holiday home; it's a whole hotel.'

Brett smiled down at her. 'Exactly. My grandparents don't do things by halves.'

Once inside the penthouse, Millie rushed to the terrace to admire the view. 'I still don't feel comfortable about this. Where are your brothers? You said Danny lives here, and Chad lives in a beach hut.'

An internal door in the penthouse flew open, and a tall young man strolled into the living area. 'You must be Millie. Grandma said you were coming for the summer.'

Brett held out his hand. 'Danny. It's good to see you, bro.'

Millie could see the family resemblance. Brett's eyelashes were longer, but they both had the same piercing green eyes and sleek black hair. However, Danny was less clean-shaven – he had designer stubble which enhanced his handsome face to perfection. Millie's knees trembled, and she sat down.

Danny laughed. 'That's great. Make yourself at home, why don't you? It's going to be a long summer.'

Millie stared at Brett, who could see her embarrassment. Brett turned to face Danny. 'I have no idea what our grandmother is concocting, but Millie is an important part of the team at *Miller, Casey & Harbottle*, and I want her returning in one piece at the end of August. I'll come back to pick her up myself.'

Millie stood up. 'Just to clarify, I don't want to be here. I'm only going through with this as I have respect for your grandmother. I've only met her briefly, but I get the impression she needs my help.' Millie waved an arm in the air. 'Come with me onto the terrace and point out where Chad lives.'

Brett and Danny duly followed and pointed to a beach house painted blue and white. Brett nodded towards it. 'It's that house over there.'

Millie raised her eyebrows. 'You said he lived in a hut.'

Brett shrugged his shoulders. 'He used to until he started selling his artwork. Now he's bought a bigger hut on the beach.'

Millie wasn't happy, and she turned to face Danny. 'It wasn't mentioned when I entered the raffle that I would be living with someone for the summer.' Millie then turned to Brett. 'It wasn't in the terms &

conditions.' Brett rubbed his chin and suppressed a smile. Millie turned back to Danny. 'I, therefore, request that you move into another room in your grandparents' hotel during my stay.'

Danny's mouth fell open, and Brett's eyes twinkled. 'Millie has a point. I'll help you move your things before I leave tonight.'

Danny turned around and stormed back into the room he'd come from before slamming the door. Brett grinned at Millie. 'You're great! Has anyone ever told you that? Let's go and grab a bite to eat while my brother licks his wounds.'

Millie's hands were shaking, and she held them behind her back. She thought back to the Easter weekend. If she hadn't watched the TV News while eating her ready meal, she wouldn't be here now. Her first thought was never to watch the TV News again. Her second thought was that she was now friends with Jordan, Brett finally knew who she was, and she didn't have a problem paying her rent – at least for the summer. A wave of calmness washed over her at her change of fortune.

9

A SEAFRONT STROLL

Millie awoke bright and early. The sun was streaming through the gap in her bedroom curtains, and she had the urge to go for an early morning stroll along the beach. It had been a taxing day yesterday, but Millie was happy with how things had turned out. Today was the first day of her summer sabbatical, and she was determined to enjoy every minute.

As she strode through the hotel foyer, the staff bowed their heads and said: 'Good morning, Miss Millie.' Millie smiled. Wilhelmina must have told them her name. No doubt Brett's grandmother would make an appearance soon. Until then, Millie was determined to keep herself entertained.

The sand between her toes felt slightly damp, and Millie stood still to watch the tide going out. She reached inside her canvas bag and pulled out her sunglasses. It was only just after seven, and Millie could tell that today was going to be a scorcher. She rummaged in her bag again and pulled out a hairband. Millie was struggling to hold everything now, so she sat down on the sea wall and placed her flip-flops, bag, and pink canvas sunhat on the sand while she tied her hair back.

With her hair suitably styled, Millie pulled her hat on and pushed her sunglasses up her nose. She shook the sand from her flip-flops and popped them in her bag. There! That was better. She'd have to get used to a different way of dressing now she was on the English Riviera. No more skirts and blouses, or trouser suits, during the day. That could be her first job; go shopping for appropriate clothes. Millie sighed; what was she doing? She was in limbo, waiting for Wilhelmina to appear, to confess why she'd been kidnapped. Maybe "kidnapped" wasn't the right word, but it felt like it – Millie had been taken away from her daily life without any choice.

Millie continued on her stroll towards Chad's beach house – her curiosity led her there. Would Chad have shiny black hair and piercing green eyes like his brothers? She hoped she'd catch a glimpse of him. She didn't need to wait long; she was ten feet away when the door to the house flew open, and two giggling girls ran out wearing bikinis. Millie strained her ears at the sound of a man's voice. What was he saying? Something about a fun night? The two girls had run into the sea and were now splashing around. The man was still talking, and Millie edged closer.

'We must do this again some time, darling. You have my number.'

Another bikini-clad girl strolled out of the house carrying a pair of flip-flops and a sarong. Millie was shocked. So Chad was a lothario! She decided to introduce herself immediately – that way, he'd know she'd witnessed three women leaving his house at the crack of dawn. Well, it was nearly eight o'clock, but it was still early.

Millie poked her head around the open door and was surprised to see that Chad didn't resemble his brothers in any way, shape, or form. He was short for a man, possibly five-foot-four, with bleached blonde dreadlocks and weather-beaten skin. She couldn't tell if he had green eyes as he was wearing sunglasses. His face lit up at the sight of her. 'Can I help you, darling?'

Millie's eyes took in the quirkiness of the beach house. It had a mezzanine floor which was Chad's living area. Millie saw a pile of washing up on the draining board, pizza boxes on the kitchen table, and a beach towel hanging from the bannisters. Downstairs was much more palatable; it housed his paintings and resembled a trendy art gallery.

It hadn't been a perfect introduction to Brett's brother – Millie instantly disliked Chad. The combination of the girls, the untidy kitchen, and the cheek to call her "darling" was just too much. She wanted to get back to the hotel as soon as possible. The only trouble was she was bound to bump into him again during the summer. Wilhelmina would probably have family dinners or invite everyone for drinks on the penthouse terrace. Millie had to be polite. 'I'm Millie. We'll no doubt meet up again soon.' Millie turned and strode back down the beach.

*

As soon as Millie reached the hotel, she went straight to her suite and opened the doors to the terrace. She'd gone off the idea of shopping for clothes. She decided to call Brett, who answered his phone straight away. 'Millie! I wasn't expecting to hear from you so soon. Why are you thinking of work?'

Millie sat down on a sun lounger and removed her flip-flops before swinging her legs onto it. 'I'm bored. When's your grandmother coming to see me?'

Brett checked his watch; he had a meeting with Jordan and *Ennis Everglades* in five minutes. 'I can't speak for long, Millie. I don't know when or if my granny will visit you.'

Millie huffed. 'I met Chad this morning. Is he adopted?'

Brett caught his breath. 'No!'

Millie tutted. 'I was surprised about his long, bleached hair and … and … his interest in the female form. He likes women, doesn't he?'

Brett smirked. 'We all like women. It's not our fault that Harbottle men are so attractive. As far as the long hair goes – Chad's an artist. What else would you expect? When he's in a zone with his work, he has no time for running a comb through his hair, he'll twist it round and hold it in place with a paintbrush. That doesn't mean he's adopted. I can't believe you said that.'

Millie could imagine the dreadlocks held together by a paintbrush; she wasn't surprised at all. Brett rechecked his watch. 'I really must go, Millie. Why don't you discover what Danny's up to with my grandparents' affairs? I'd be interested to know what keeps him busy for the whole week. You can update me later.'

Brett ended the call, and Millie swung her legs off the sun lounger to witness an interior door of the penthouse opening and Danny walking through it. Her blood pressure rose. She ran inside to face him. 'I asked you to find another room. I said I won't be living with you for the summer.'

Danny grinned. 'I *have* found another room. I slept there last night; I'm going back there now to get a bottle of water out of the minibar. It's only a small room, there were no suites available, so I'll have to make do without a kitchen area or a balcony while you enjoy your raffle prize.'

Millie folded her arms. 'But you just came out of that room over there.'

Danny waved a key in the air. 'That's my place of work. You can't stop me from doing my job. I'll need to walk through the penthouse to get there each day during the week. I won't be bothering you at weekends. Now, if you let me pass, I'll pop out to get a drink and make sure I'm fully stocked up each day so that I only have to leave my place of work for lunch. My hours of work are nine to five with lunch from one to two. If you remember that, we can avoid each other all summer.'

Millie frowned. 'What about the toilet?'

Danny nodded towards the closed door. 'My office was originally a bedroom. It has an en-suite bathroom.'

Millie felt thankful for that. She was surprised Danny was being so accommodating. 'Wait there.'

Millie walked into the kitchen and returned with two bottles of water. 'These should keep you going until lunchtime.'

10

ALL'S NOT AS IT SEEMS

Jordan knocked on Brett's office door before opening it. '*Ennis Everglades* are here.'

Brett stood up and grabbed his jacket. 'I'm not looking forward to this after the way your meeting went with them yesterday. I'm sure they're going to cancel our contract.' Jordan pulled a worried face, and Brett continued, 'Settle them in the boardroom with some drinks. I have a quick call to make before I join you.'

Jordan nodded and closed the door. Brett strode to the window and stared out of it as he made the call. 'Chad! Good to speak to you, bro. I take it you're away at some flashy art festival ... Cannes? ... Lucky you, I'm about to go into a meeting to get beaten up ... Anyway, it sounds like Zane is using your beachside studio as a love nest again … Oh, and Millie is staying in the penthouse for the summer … Millie? … She's one of our recruitment administrators … I don't have time now to go into detail … What? … You're back in Devon on Saturday? … I may pop down and see you. It's been ages since we met up.'

*

It was twelve-forty-five. Millie finished her lunch and grabbed her bag; she'd go shopping before Danny surfaced. She strode through the hotel foyer to the usual polite greetings from the staff. The heat hit her when she stepped onto the promenade, and she pulled on her hat. Millie lowered her sunglasses. Chad was sitting on a bench, minus his shirt, eating a jumbo-sized sausage roll. She guessed he needed the energy. She sighed when she thought of his poor grandmother. Millie couldn't imagine Wilhelmina being impressed with his harem of girls or the state he kept his art studio in. She couldn't help herself from going over to speak to him.

He recognised her straight away. 'Hi, Millie. What are you up to this afternoon? Fancy a spot of surfing later?'

Millie cringed at the thought. 'No, I don't. I do have the afternoon to spare, though, and I really can't believe I'm about to say this, but I feel it's my duty to come back with you to the beach house and tidy up your living accommodation.'

Chad choked on his sausage roll before doing his best to keep a straight face. 'Well, the place could do with a good clean before the weekend.' He reached into his pocket for a set of keys. 'Here, help yourself. I have plans for this afternoon. Just leave the keys at the reception desk in the hotel over there when you've finished. They'll know what to do with them.' Chad stood up and waved to Millie as he headed towards the pier. He shook his head; some girls were really weird.

At first, Millie was livid. But, if she were honest with herself, she'd rather do the cleaning on her own. There was a good chance that Wilhelmina would turn up soon, and at least her grandson wouldn't be seen in such a bad light if she made an effort to tidy his studio.

Millie turned the key in the lock of the beach house door and switched on the lights. There was a selection to choose from; she pressed each one in turn. Some lit up the paintings, and others gave off coloured hues to change the ambience in the room. Millie gasped when she pressed the final switch; an array of fairy lights lit up the mezzanine floor. She was surprised at Chad's great taste. Millie was even more astounded when she surveyed the paintings. She'd imagined they'd be the type of abstract art she always thought she could do better herself, particularly after Brett portrayed Chad with a paintbrush in his hair. But she was wrong; the paintings could only be described as fine art.

Millie was shocked. She wandered around the gallery in a trance for ten minutes before her mind returned to the job at hand – she was here to clean up. As Millie climbed the stairs to the living area, she could see that the kitchen was spotless. Millie felt very rude. How could she tell Chad his place needed cleaning when she'd only seen it early in the morning, and he hadn't had a chance to do it himself? Apart from being her boss's brother, he was also a very talented man. Instead of "fitting in" on the English Riviera, she was sticking out like a sore thumb and falling out with Brett's brothers along the way. There was nothing else for it – retail therapy was required.

*

It was four-forty before Millie returned to the penthouse suite armed with bags of shoes and dresses; she'd also bought a red straw hat to go with the off-the-shoulder dress she'd found in a little boutique up a side street in the main shopping area. Millie had made a note that market days were on Wednesdays and Saturdays. At least she'd have somewhere to go tomorrow. It was good to have a plan. Danny's door opened, and Millie threw herself on the sofa with her back to his office. 'Don't worry, Danny. Just pretend I'm not here. I forgot the time.'

Danny couldn't resist a smirk as he strolled past

behind the sofa. 'Have a good evening.'

'You, too.'

Millie heard the door to the penthouse close, and she jumped up to unload the food shopping she'd bought into the fridge. Her heart sank as she lifted a microwavable spaghetti bolognese out of the carrier bag. That was tonight's dinner – another ready meal for one. She suddenly felt very lonely. She was more alone now than when Shelley had moved out of her apartment. At least, back home, she had the girls at work to chat to, and she'd enjoyed becoming friends with Brett and Jordan. This raffle prize wasn't turning out to be much fun at all. A call from Jordan broke her thoughts. 'Hi, Millie. I hope you've had a better day than us.'

Millie stepped onto the terrace and looked out to sea while she listened to Jordan's solemn voice. 'As we thought, *Ennis Everglades* have pulled the plug on us. It was Sadie's charm that held that account together. Also, two of the recruitment consultants won't sign their new contracts, so they're leaving at the end of the month. Brett will give you all the details when he speaks to you.'

Millie was aghast; she didn't know what to say. 'Have *you* signed your new contract?'

'I told you; I can't commit to six months. I can't

tell Brett yet; he's in a bit of a state. He stormed out of the office mid-afternoon. You should let him tell you about *Ennis Everglades*. I was trying to give you the heads up, so it's not such a shock.'

'Why can't you commit to six months?'

Jordan sighed. 'I never should have told you. Just forget I mentioned it. The main thing is that we help Brett through this crisis at work.'

11

A HEADY EXPERIENCE

Millie sat on the terrace, with the doors closed, until nine-fifteen. She checked the time on her phone. Danny would be in his office by now. She couldn't believe that *Miller, Casey & Harbottle* had lost the *Ennis Everglades* contract. She'd put so much work into it with Jordan when Sadie had gone to Paris for a jolly. Unfortunately, *Picard Ratcliffe* had offered Sadie a job, and that's when the wheels on *Miller, Casey & Harbottle's* recruitment business had begun to fall off.

Millie opened the terrace doors and stepped inside the penthouse; her mind was spinning. There must be something she could do to help. Brett had left the office early yesterday, and he hadn't contacted her to tell her the bad news. Jordan sounded worried he also had a plan that he wouldn't divulge. Things couldn't get much worse. Millie decided to go for a walk to clear her head.

*

Millie strode along the promenade, oblivious of her surroundings, until she reached the market. When she lifted her head, she caught her breath at the abundance of colourful stalls of local produce. She felt revitalised – until she realised Chad was watching her. He was working on a fruit and veg stall. 'Well, well, well; it's Millie again. Thank you for offering to do a spot of cleaning for me yesterday. By the way, I won't need your services for a while. I'm moving further down the coast for the summer. I'll be off on Monday.'

Millie felt her head was going to burst. What was Chad doing working on the market? She needed to make up with him soon if he was going away. 'I feel embarrassed; you'd tidied up yourself. I didn't have any cleaning to do. I apologise for interfering. I hope we can part ways as friends.'

Chad's brown eyes twinkled beneath his sunglasses. 'How about dinner on Saturday night?'

Millie frowned; she didn't feel comfortable with that. There was safety in numbers, though, and she had an idea. 'That would be great. Come to the penthouse at seven o'clock, and I'll order room service. We can eat on the terrace.'

Chad raised his eyebrows. 'What penthouse?'

Millie nodded back towards the hotel. 'I'm staying in the penthouse at the hotel.' She was surprised that Chad didn't know.

Chad smiled. 'See you at seven on Saturday then, darling.'

Millie shivered. Did he really have to call her that?! Still, she'd only have to put up with him for one evening. She turned and headed up a small side street away from his gaze. When Millie reached a clearing at the top of a hill, she sat on a bench overlooking the sea and phoned Brett. She was surprised when he answered straight away. 'Hello Brett, I don't know all the details of what's happening at the office – you can tell me in your own time. I was calling to see if you're available on Saturday night to come for dinner at the penthouse. Chad will be there, and I'd prefer it if you could join us. You can have a brotherly catch-up.'

Brett caught his breath. Chad hadn't wasted any time introducing himself to Millie; he must have called her from Cannes. Brett wasn't surprised Millie felt uncomfortable about having dinner with a man she hadn't met. 'I'll drive down on Saturday morning and stay over in the hotel.'

Millie let out a sigh of relief. 'That's great, thanks, Brett. Dinner's at seven.'

There was a magnificent view of the coastline from the top of the hill, and Millie decided to walk further along the coastal path. She strode along with the wind in her hair and her head spinning. It wasn't until Millie felt an acute pang of hunger that she checked the time on her phone. She'd been walking for over two hours and could no longer see the sea. Millie had headed inland and was now at the entrance to a business park. Her heart sank – no pasty shop, ice-cream van or public toilet in sight.

Millie looked down at her feet. She was wearing trainers today, that's why she'd been able to walk so far. Her floral maxi dress lifted in the breeze, and, although she'd remembered her sunglasses, she'd forgotten to wear her hat. She looked a mess as she stood outside a portacabin containing a security guard who peered out of a window. 'Are you here for the recruitment day at *Mosely Timmins*?' Millie took a step backwards before nodding. 'Here's a Visitor Pass. Head down to the roundabout, turn right, and it's the first building on the left.'

Millie clipped the pass to her dress and thanked her lucky stars. At least she'd be able to use the toilet before her trek back down the hill. If the recruitment day was organised to the standard of ones she'd been involved with in the past, there was a good chance she'd get a sandwich too.

Millie stood in front of the tall white building

admiring the shiny gold *Mosely Timmins* lettering. There was a desk in the foyer with a banner:

RECRUITMENT DAY

Millie looked around before receiving a tap on her shoulder. 'You're early, aren't you? This morning's session still has half an hour to run. Take a seat, and I'll find you a welcome pack to read through while you're waiting.'

Millie smiled at the smartly-dressed woman whose name badge read: *Cynthia Althorpe, HR Director – Mosely Timmins.* Cynthia returned with a pack, and Millie scanned through it with interest. *Mosely Timmins* were investment bankers who were expanding into Europe. They had twenty-five vacancies for a variety of finance roles. Millie popped the pack in her bag and went to the toilet; she couldn't possibly pose as a finance candidate in her floral dress and trainers. She'd make a quick exit as soon as Cynthia was out of the way.

Unfortunately, Cynthia didn't get out of the way. She was pacing up and down in the foyer when Millie opened the cloakroom door. 'Not long to go now. The first session is almost over. Which of the finance roles are you interested in?'

Millie didn't get a chance to answer as Cynthia was tapped on the shoulder by a tall woman in a pinstripe trouser suit. 'How's it gone this morning? Good, I hope. Make sure you see me later today. We need to start the recruitment drive for the marketing and sales professionals there's no time to waste.'

Millie saw the colour drain from Cynthia's face. 'My team are working overtime already. We'll never cope.'

The tall woman in the trouser suit smiled. 'Oh, yes, you will.' Millie caught sight of her name badge, which read: *Helga Hanscombe – Chief Executive – Mosely Timmins.*

Helga shot up the stairs, two at a time, and Cynthia turned back to face Millie. She forced a smile. 'Sorry about that. As I was saying, which finance role are you interested in?'

Millie blushed. 'None of them. I only wanted to use the toilet and possibly buy a sandwich. I got lost on my way up the hill. There's so much going on at the moment. My head was spinning, and I lost track of time . . . and where I was going.'

Cynthia smiled. 'Tell me about it; my team's never been so busy. There's a buffet lunch laid on in the auditorium for the delegates. Why don't you pop in there and take a sandwich or two for your walk home.'

Millie was bursting with an idea. 'Thank you. If you don't mind me saying, you should consider outsourcing the recruitment side of your role. That would free you and your team up to work on all the other challenges with the expansion of *Mosely Timmins* into Europe. You'll still have all the employment contracts to produce and induction programmes to undertake. You'll never cope. You need an expert recruitment team to source all the candidates and provide you with a shortlist of the cream of the crop.'

Cynthia sighed. 'I wish. But things are happening so quickly I don't have time to source a reliable organisation. Besides, we won't find one that can work with us at the drop of a hat.'

Millie was feeling brave. 'I have a perfect solution for you. I'm a recruitment administrator, and I'm available all summer. If you have a spare desk I could use to help your team with the workload, then I'm at your disposal. Of course, you'll need the services of more than just an administrator to complete the mammoth task before you. That's where the company I work for comes in. *Miller, Casey & Harbottle* are at the top of their game. You won't find a more professional recruitment agency. If you're interested, I'll call my boss now. I'm sure he'd love to meet you.'

Cynthia had nothing to lose. Besides, she liked the boldness of this young woman who may have saved her from a nervous breakdown. 'OK, call your boss, and I'll collect you a plate of food before it all goes.'

Brett was dumbfounded. 'You're an angel. No, you're my fairy godmother! Advise Cynthia I'll drive down to Devon tonight. I'll be available any time she can make tomorrow or Friday.' Brett checked his watch. 'Traffic permitting, I'll be with you by seven. I'll buy you dinner.'

12

BACK DOWN TO EARTH

The walk back down the hill was delightful. Millie felt ten feet tall. She took her time to enjoy the view of the coastline and sat on the same bench she'd stopped at earlier to reflect on the surprising chain of events. There was no guarantee her idea would get off the ground, but Brett sounded hopeful. Maybe this was why she was meant to spend the summer in Devon; she was sent here to save *Miller, Casey & Harbottle*. Millie chuckled to herself; her imagination ran riot sometimes. Still, if she hadn't had the unbridled urge to articulate her suggestion to Cynthia, Brett wouldn't be taking her out for dinner later, and she'd be wandering around the English Riviera like a lost soul until September.

As Millie watched the yachts gliding around on the

ocean, a wave of calmness washed over her. She didn't know why, but something about this felt right. She closed her eyes and wished with all her heart that she could save *Miller, Casey & Harbottle* from folding after Sadie's exit and the mess with all the contracts. Jordan had sounded defeated yesterday. He'd also sounded very worried about Brett.

Millie's reflective moment was shattered by a hand touching her shoulder. 'Are you having a sleep, my dear?'

Millie recognised the voice straight away, and she jumped up off the bench. 'Madame Wilhelmina! I've been waiting for you to turn up. You'll never guess what's just happened! You brought me down here to save your grandson's business, didn't you? Well, I may be onto something that will dig Brett out of a hole.'

Wilhelmina kept a straight face; Millie was an astute girl. She forced a smile before responding, 'Not at all, dear. Brett's old enough to sort out his own problems.'

Millie frowned. If Brett didn't need her, she must be here to help Chad or Danny. Her best guess was that Chad needed sorting out, but he was going away on Monday for the summer. If Danny needed help, that would be pretty difficult to establish while they were avoiding one another.

Millie held her hands in the air. 'Please tell me why I'm here?'

Wilhelmina smiled. 'It's simple. You won the raffle.'

Millie sighed; things were never that simple. Something strange was going on. She was beginning to get annoyed with the older woman, but she couldn't "lose" her again. Wilhelmina would confess what was going on at some stage. Millie had a thought. 'Come to the penthouse for dinner on Saturday night. Chad and Brett will be there and … and … maybe Danny too.'

Wilhelmina's green eyes twinkled. 'How wonderful! All of my grandsons together at once! How can I refuse? What time should I appear, my dear?'

*

Millie trudged down the hill while Wilhelmina departed in the opposite direction. Millie felt a knot in her stomach. Anxiety kicked in when she thought about inviting Danny to the dinner – what if he refused?

*

At five o'clock, the door to Danny's place of work opened. He was surprised to see Millie waiting outside. Millie held her shoulders back before speaking, 'I'm having a dinner party on Saturday evening. Chad, Brett, and your grandmother will be coming. It would give your grandmother great pleasure to have all of her grandsons together at once. It is for that reason you are invited to attend.'

Danny rubbed his chin as he stared into Millie's cornflower blue eyes. He was taken aback; he hadn't bothered to look at her in any detail before. She was beautiful; she should wear her long raven hair down more often. He closed his office door and locked it while considering his response. Millie saw he was nervous; his hands were shaking as he fiddled with the key. 'Well, Danny? Will you be coming to dinner or not?'

Danny's phone rang, and he stared at Millie as he answered it. 'Yes, it's Danny Harbottle … What? Another five thousand words by Monday? … I'll need to work all weekend … No, I understand … You're a slave driver … I know – no pain, no gain.' Danny ended the call and shoved his phone in his pocket before staring at Millie. 'What time is the dinner on Saturday?'

Millie was shocked, it sounded like Danny had a good excuse not to attend, so she was surprised he was asking the time. 'Seven o'clock. Look, it sounds like you're busy. If you need to use your office over the weekend, just come and go as you please.'

Danny wound his way past her before turning to look over his shoulder. 'I'll be at the dinner. Thanks for allowing me to use my office over the weekend, but I won't be inconveniencing you a moment longer than is necessary.'

The door to the penthouse closed, and Millie turned to face Danny's office. The key was still in the door. She felt a pang of guilt. She wanted to look inside, but she shouldn't, should she? Besides, Danny may realise he'd left the key and come straight back. Millie walked out onto the terrace and took a deep breath of sea air before she noticed Danny striding down the promenade. She ran back to his office and turned the key in the lock.

*

Danny was headed for the pier. His phone rang again. 'Hi, Grandma ... that's right ... I finished the accounts yesterday ... no, I don't have a girlfriend yet ... I don't have time ... of course, I'll be at the dinner on Saturday ... I wouldn't miss it for the world.'

*

Millie couldn't believe her eyes – Chad wasn't the only artist in the family. There were sketches all over the place. Unlike Chad's fine art paintings, Danny's drawings were whimsical. Millie would never have guessed there was such a colourful side to Brett's moody brother. It sounded like he wrote stories too. "Another five thousand words by Monday" sprang to mind. Brett had asked Millie to establish what Danny was doing – but she couldn't tell him about this. Danny was moonlighting. He was doing a job for his grandparents and working as an author and artist at the same time. Millie closed his office door, turned the key, and left it in the lock.

13

MIRACULOUS MILLIE

Brett bounded into the penthouse suite just before seven, armed with flowers. Millie was wearing a white broderie anglaise dress with her hair piled on top of her head. Brett extracted a pink rose before shortening the stem and sticking it behind her ear. 'There! A perfect picture of miraculous Millie!'

Mille laughed. 'I've done nothing.'

Brett shoved the flowers into her arms. 'You may have saved our organisation. Working with *Mosely Timmins* will keep us ticking by until we pick up more lucrative contracts. Our business has every chance of expanding with people like you on our team.'

Millie walked into the kitchen area to find a vase. 'It's not a done deal. Cynthia Althorpe has only agreed to an initial meeting with you.'

Brett winked. 'At nine o'clock tomorrow morning. That shows she's keen.'

Millie cut the stems of the flowers as she placed them in the vase. 'Cynthia's nice, but Helga Hanscombe won't be easily won round.'

Brett frowned. 'The Chief Exec? Just leave her to me. I got Melanie to do a profile check on her. I know what buttons to push when we meet in the morning. Hopefully, you've brought some work clothes with you; we'll need to look professional.'

Millie looked down at her white dress. She had smart trousers and a blouse in the wardrobe – they would have to do. She needed to confess to Brett what was worrying her, 'I offered to help *Mosely Timmins* out and work for them over the summer. It took me hours to walk to their office building – I went off track. I don't have a car; there's no public transport . . .' Millie lowered her head before continuing, 'I've been foolish.'

Brett grinned. 'You caught their attention; that's the main thing. You showed passion and commitment – that's what I need from my team. Don't worry about the detail; I just need you to partner me in the morning – I'll take the lead. You won't be working for them all summer; my granny won't allow it.'

Millie's eyes widened. 'Why won't your

grandmother allow it?'

Brett sighed. 'She has other plans for you. I'm not happy about that, but what Granny wants, Granny gets.'

*

Brett and Millie sat in the boardroom at *Mosely Timmins*, making polite conversation with Cynthia Althorpe. Before long, Helga Hanscombe pushed the meeting room door open and strode over to shake hands. 'I'm Helga Hanscombe, Chief Executive. I'm not sure why my HR Director needs to outsource our recruitment requirements.' Helga directed her squint towards Brett. '*You* will need to convince me if this is a worthwhile opportunity for our business or not.'

Brett picked up a plate of biscuits. 'I rather like jammy dodgers, don't you? There's so much more to them than people realise.'

Helga shifted in her seat. 'I prefer plain digestives. What you see is what you get.'

Millie cringed; this wasn't starting well. Brett bit into a jammy dodger, then licked his lips. 'If this biscuit were a candidate, it would have many layers. It takes someone of my experience to identify that.' Brett then picked up a plain digestive. 'If this were a candidate, it would be shallow and boring. The employees you recruit need room to grow. That way, you can mould them into the *Mosely Timmins* culture and, in turn, utilise their strengths to enhance your business.'

Helga uncrossed her legs, then crossed them again before folding her arms. Millie saw Cynthia hold a hand over her mouth. Brett continued, 'Only a seasoned sailor could stand at the helm of a multi-national business and steer it into safe waters and beyond. A business like *Mosely Timmins* has an ocean of wealth just waiting for those fishing nets to be dropped and the catch, or rather cash, to be reeled in.'

Helga glared at Brett. 'I have to give it to you; you've done some research. However, my sailing experience is not on fishing boats; I'm an expert kayaker. What do you have to say about that?'

Brett reached for a glass of water – Melanie had made him look like a fool. That was the last time he'd ask *her* to do any research. Millie noticed Brett's awkwardness, and she smiled at Helga. 'Being a kayaker, you'll notice the detail and spot things that other sailors don't. You'll manoeuvre through challenging rivers and even tackle rapids. It's mind-boggling what kayakers do.'

Brett nudged his leg against Millie's. He needed to stop her there; this was turning into a farce. Helga stood up before scowling at Cynthia. 'What a waste of my time!'

Brett pulled a leaflet out of his folder and handed it to Helga. 'Here's a list of our clients. We're very selective about who we work with. Due to our success, we have the luxury of being able to choose the most prestigious organisations.'

Helga scanned the list. 'I see you work with *Picard Ratcliffe* - they're major players in the dog food world. My Pomeranians adore their Celebrity Canine Crunchies.'

Millie lowered her eyes, and Brett kept a straight face. It wasn't *his* fault they hadn't had new promotional leaflets printed yet. That would be a job for Melanie when he returned to the office. Brett closed his folder and stood up too. He held out his hand to shake Helga's. 'It's been a pleasure meeting you. We must be off now as we have an appointment with a major conglomerate this afternoon.' Brett tapped his nose. 'If I gave you the name, I'd be locked away – Official Secrets Act and all that.'

Helga's mouth fell open, and she stared at Brett to gauge his response to her question, 'Do you regard *Mosely Timmins* as a prestigious organisation?'

Brett nodded. 'Of course, otherwise, I wouldn't be here today wasting my time.' He paused to give his brightest smile to the iron woman. There it was – she was starting to melt; he could now go in for the kill. 'We're here to help you, Helga. I can't give you Millie for the summer, but I *can* provide a whole team of experts who will work around the clock to meet your recruitment deadlines. If we join together, *Mosely Timmins* will have the best opportunity to break into Europe and beyond. We're ready for the challenge. Are you?'

Helga held her shoulders back. 'Of course, let's get started. Cynthia will be your direct contact. She will keep me informed of progress.'

Helga left the room, and Cynthia held out her hand to shake Millie's and Brett's. 'Don't let me down.'

Brett squeezed Cynthia's hand. 'We won't.'

*

Millie and Brett were back at the penthouse by twelve-forty-five. Millie opened the doors to the terrace and signalled for Brett to take a seat on one of the sun loungers. 'I'll make us a sandwich.'

Brett raised his eyebrows. 'What's the rush?'

Millie grabbed two cans of lemonade out of the fridge and placed them on a tray with two ham sandwiches, and a packet of crisps, before meeting the one o'clock deadline. She handed the tray to Brett and closed the terrace doors. Brett noticed his brother exit his office, and he frowned at Millie. 'Are you avoiding Danny?'

Millie blushed. 'Let's just say we have an "arrangement". We didn't get off to a very good start.'

Brett bit into his sandwich. 'Have you worked out yet what Danny's up to?'

Millie shook her head. Hopefully, Danny hadn't thought more about leaving the key in the lock. She guessed he was relieved that it was still there and presumed she hadn't noticed. Luckily she'd left the penthouse well before nine this morning – it was best to keep a distance from Brett's moody brother.

14

JUST ANOTHER SATURDAY

Saturday had arrived, and Millie decided to take a trip to the market to buy flowers for tonight. The hotel staff were setting up a table for dinner on the penthouse terrace, with the meal scheduled for seven o'clock. Until then, Millie was at a loss, so buying flowers and arranging them would give her something to do. Brett was shut away in his hotel room working on the *Mosely Timmins* contract, and Danny was busy too – although, even if he wasn't, Millie guessed their paths wouldn't cross unless absolutely necessary.

Chad was, again, working on a fruit and veg stall; he waved to her. 'Hey, darling! You couldn't do me a favour, could you?'

Millie sighed, surely Chad should be working in his gallery trying to sell paintings? She looked at him over her sunglasses. 'What's that?'

'I left my pen in the beach house, and I can't go away without it. You couldn't pop down there, could you, and pick it up for me?'

Millie frowned. 'You're not going away until Monday. Can't you get it yourself?'

Chad grinned. 'I'm a bit busy, darling. I'm working here today; I have a hot date tonight, and tomorrow, I plan to catch some waves.'

Millie couldn't stand this man. How could he possibly be related to Brett or even the moody Danny? Wilhelmina must be at her wit's end with this grandson of hers. Suddenly any excitement Millie had felt about tonight's dinner party turned to anxiety.

Chad was persistent. 'Well, are you going to help me? You can pick the keys up from the hotel reception, and you'll find my pen on the coffee table. You won't miss it; it's in the shape of a green snake with wobbly red eyes. I've had it for years; it goes everywhere with me.'

Millie was becoming annoyed. 'Surely you can pick it up tonight? Hopefully, you'll be getting changed before dinner.'

Chad shook his head. 'I'm not going back to the beach house again; I'm staying in my camper van. Don't worry; I'll go for a swim and put on some clean shorts before I meet you for our hot date.'

Millie cringed. 'OK. I'll go and get your pen. And if a meal with your brothers and grandmother is classed as a hot date, then your love life must have hit rock bottom.'

*

Millie unlocked the beach house and switched on the lights. She was fuming. Thank goodness Chad was going away. She headed up the stairs to the mezzanine floor and spotted the snake pen on the coffee table; she picked it up and shoved it in her bag before climbing back down the stairs.

Chad's paintings were stunning; Millie couldn't resist walking around the gallery while she studied each one. The sound of the exterior door opening broke her thoughts. 'Hello. I'm afraid we're not open. I'm only here doing a favour for the artist.' Millie continued to view the artwork. 'The paintings are amazing, aren't they? If you like, I could give Chad Harbottle your name and number, and he can contact you to arrange a meeting. He's going further down the coast on Monday for the summer in his camper van. Do you have a painting in mind?'

Millie turned her focus away from the paintings to see a tall, dark-haired man wearing designer sunglasses standing next to a flight bag. She held out her hand. 'I'm sorry for being so rude. My name's Millie, and I'm a friend of the family.'

Millie felt the smoothness of the man's hand while admiring his manicured nails and tanned skin. 'Have you just got off a plane?'

The man nodded, and Millie caught a whiff of expensive aftershave. 'I flew in from France this morning.'

Sunglasses or not, Millie felt his gaze bore into her. She struggled to know what to say. 'Well, I would highly recommend the hotel over the road. I'm staying in the penthouse suite for the summer. I won a raffle prize and ended up here. Madame Wilhelmina insisted I came. Her grandson, Brett, is my boss. To be honest, I'm a bit in limbo. Anyway, enough about me. If you could just let me have your name and number and an idea of which painting you prefer, then I'll pass the information on.'

The man produced a pen and paper from his jacket pocket and scribbled on it before passing the note to Millie:

ZANE – 07795-984291

Millie smiled. 'That's great. Oh, and which painting do you like best?'

The man flashed a perfect white smile. 'I like all of them. I don't have a favourite.'

The man exited the beach house, and Millie held a

hand to her chest. Wow! That man had "presence". He must be big in the art world. Chad did not deserve to be mixing with people like that. Millie locked the beach house and headed back to the market. This time she would hand over the name and number to Chad, with a brief description of the man, along with the snake pen. After that, she would search for flowers and try to make the rest of the day as pleasant as possible.

*

"Chad" read the name and number while he listened to Millie's account of his potential customer from the art world. Things were going from bad to worse. He'd been an innocent bystander in all of this until meddling Millie had trapped him in a tangled web of mistaken identity. It all made sense now; it wasn't *his* grandmother and brothers going to the dinner tonight (thank goodness). Millie had mistaken him for Chad, who was now back and firing a warning shot at him by calling himself "Zane".

Without the potential hot date tonight, and the risk of the Harbottle clan boxing his ears, Zane needed to make a quick getaway. As soon as Millie was out of sight, he headed for his camper van. After throwing his pen into the glove compartment, Zane wound down the windows, turned on the ignition and headed down the coast.

15

DINNER AT THE PENTHOUSE

Brett sat in the hotel bar with Danny. He'd tried to contact Chad, but he wasn't answering his phone. He finished his beer and then glanced over at his brother. 'Want another one? It's only six-forty-five.'

Danny placed his empty glass on the table. 'Go on then. It'll help take the edge off the atmosphere in the penthouse suite. You could cut it with a knife. I don't like that girl; she's spying on me. Why else would our grandmother set her up for a summer of luxury in the family holiday home?'

Brett shifted in his seat. He'd been the one to ask Millie to keep an eye on Danny. Although Brett was trying to be civilised with his brother, it didn't take away from the fact he was lazy and living off their grandparents; that riled Brett to the core. Two more beers arrived, and Brett couldn't help himself. 'When are you going to get your own place? You must realise everyone looks down on you. You're twenty-eight and sponging off our grandparents while Chad and I work our butts off. Well, just me, really. Chad has an easy life too.'

Wilhelmina tutted as she stood behind a pillar in the bar. She took a deep breath and then walked over to her grandsons. 'Drinking already? I suggest we head up now; we wouldn't want to keep Millie waiting. It's been very kind of her to arrange a family get-together.'

Wilhelmina glanced at Brett hanging his head in the lift. No doubt worried she'd overheard his comments. Brett needed to be careful; Wilhelmina had propped him up throughout his career – *she* was the "Harbottle" in *Miller, Casey & Harbottle*. Brett had just got lucky. She was annoyed her eldest grandson was being hard on her youngest.

Millie was standing on the penthouse terrace wringing her hands together when she saw Wilhelmina enter with Brett and Danny. Wilhelmina walked up to her and kissed her on both cheeks. 'This is so wonderful, Millie. I hope you haven't gone to too much trouble.'

Millie blushed. 'Oh, I've done nothing, except arrange a few flowers from the market. I needed to keep busy.'

Brett walked over and kissed Millie on her cheek. 'Thanks for arranging this. I can't remember the last time we all got together.'

Wilhelmina could; it was five Christmases ago. She'd done her best to keep her grandsons together after their parents split up, but her family was falling apart. It had been very upsetting for the boys when their mother emigrated to Australia with a toyboy younger than them, and their father moved to Canada with an opera-singing tree surgeon.

As the family's matriarch, Wilhelmina was under pressure. She was concerned Brett's business wasn't doing well. She was also annoyed he held a grudge against his younger brothers. Danny was becoming a recluse, and that broke Wilhelmina's heart. How could she break down the wall he'd erected around himself since his parents' divorce? Then there was Chad. A twinkle came into Wilhelmina's eyes; she couldn't find fault with Chad.

Danny rubbed at the stubble on his chin before holding a chair out for his grandmother. He glanced at Millie then sat down. Brett held out a chair for Millie. When everyone was seated, a member of staff appeared. 'One guest is missing. Shall we serve the starter, or would you like to wait?'

Millie was annoyed. Chad was so unreliable; he'd probably lost track of the time when he went for his swim. 'Please serve the starter, thank you. Our guest can catch up when he gets here.'

Wilhelmina and Brett raised their eyebrows, and Millie continued, 'There's no way we're waiting for Chad. I'm sorry, Wilhelmina, but your artist grandson isn't a gentleman like these two sitting here.' Brett burst out laughing, and Danny blushed. Millie opened her arms out wide. 'Look around. We're here in such a perfect setting on the English Riviera, and Chad would rather be playing with his snake in his camper van.'

There was a flash from a camera, and Millie looked up to see the man from this morning. He took off his sunglasses, revealing his brilliant green eyes. 'That's a perfect shot of a passionate woman. With your permission, I will paint it on canvas.'

Millie threw a hand to her mouth, and Brett worked out what was happening. Only Zane would be playing with a snake in a camper van. Millie had well and truly got hold of the wrong end of the stick. He couldn't believe she hadn't worked out the case of mistaken identity from earlier in the week.

The man walked over to kiss Wilhelmina. 'Hello, Grandma, it's good to see you.' He then held out his hand to shake Millie's. 'I'm sorry to add to the confusion, Millie, but when I saw you in my gallery this morning, I was stunned. It soon became apparent that you thought Zane was me. I'd spoken to Brett earlier in the week, and he advised me that Zane had been using the beach house while I was away. Brett also mentioned you're staying here for the summer. I needed time to get my head around things before coming here tonight.'

Millie gasped. 'How did you know about the dinner party?'

'I've had several messages from Brett.' Chad glanced at his brother. 'Apologies for not responding, but I was in a meeting all afternoon.'

Millie was horrified; she'd never been so embarrassed in her life. She pushed her chair back. 'Excuse me. This is all a bit too much. I'm sorry for getting things so wrong.'

Danny noticed tears welling in Millie's eyes and he pushed his chair back too. 'I'll go after her.'

Wilhelmina's heart was warmed at Danny's concern for Millie. 'I suggest you take her down to the bar and buy her a stiff drink – make sure you have one too. We'll hold the main course until you're back. Now, Chad, tell me all about Cannes.'

*

Millie sipped the brandy Danny had bought her. 'Ergh! This is gross.'

Danny sipped his too. 'I agree. Let's get them

down us; it's Grandma's idea.'

A group of people entered the bar, and Millie jerked before grabbing Danny's hand. 'You don't think Zane will turn up too, do you?'

Danny glanced down at Millie's hand in his. That was a surprise; a smile touched his lips, and his green eyes twinkled as he locked eyes with his former sparring partner. 'No – I saw his camper van leave when I was on my way to the pier earlier. I couldn't miss it. The windows were down, and he was singing along to some rap music.'

Millie giggled. 'Thank goodness for that. I can't believe I've been such a fool. What must Chad think of me?'

Danny finished his brandy before responding, 'He thinks he's found his latest muse.'

'What's a muse?'

'A source of inspiration.'

Millie finished her drink too. 'Wow! I feel much better after that brandy. We should get back to the penthouse. It's sea bass for the main course.'

*

Chad stood up at the sight of Millie returning to the terrace. Wilhelmina wasn't surprised by Chad's good manners. She *was* surprised when Danny escorted Millie to her seat and held her chair out for her. That was an improvement from the start of the meal. Danny also had a smile on his face. He was far more handsome when he smiled. Millie could be the one to bring him out of his shell. Wilhelmina felt a sense of satisfaction. Things were falling into place.

By the end of the main course, Wilhelmina could contain her plans no longer. She caught Brett's eye. 'As you know, I am a sleeping partner in your business. Well, Danny's been doing a lot of work for me behind the scenes, and with his astute legal and financial expertise, I am no longer sleeping. I'm flying high! We've bought out the Miller and Casey shareholders, and from next week, *Miller, Casey & Harbottle* will become the *Harbottle Recruitment Agency*. We'll keep the business for now, although I know it's struggling. We'll also be changing the hotel's name to the *Harbottle Harbourside Hotel* and undertaking a complete refurbishment.'

Brett glared at Danny. 'You didn't mention any of this.'

Danny shrugged his shoulders. 'It wasn't my place.'

Brett frowned. How had Wilhelmina got such an injection of cash? Brett knew Danny had a law degree, but he thought he was squandering his qualifications, while plodding along working for his grandparents. In Brett's eyes, Danny had always been a loser. Maybe there was more to his youngest brother than he realised.

Chad's attention was on Millie. 'You have such great bone structure. I want to take images of you in different locations on the English Riviera and then bring you to life on canvas. If you agree, *Millie's Summer Collection* will be ready for launch by the beginning of August at my gallery in London. I'll, of course, pay you a modelling fee.'

Millie gasped. 'That's less than two months away. Can you do paintings that quickly? Isn't your diary full already?'

Wilhelmina smiled at her artist grandson before turning to Millie. 'Chad is a master in his field. When he sets his mind to something, there's no stopping him. I think *Millie's Summer Collection* will be a fun thing for you to work on together. Will you do it?'

Millie felt excited, but Brett didn't need to know that. She could feel his agitation from across the table. Danny had already predicted this, and he gave her a knowing grin. Millie felt a bit guilty about leaving a sinking Brett to work with high-flying Chad, but Brett had turned her offer of help down. She feigned a sigh before responding, 'If I must.'

16

HELP NEEDED

Brett bounded into the penthouse suite at nine o'clock; Millie was eating her breakfast on the terrace. She turned to look at him. 'Nice of you to knock.'

Brett frowned. 'Danny doesn't knock when he comes and goes. I've noticed that.'

Millie put a strawberry back on her plate. 'That's during the week when he needs to get to work. He doesn't come here at weekends.' Millie could see a redness creeping up Brett's neck, and she decided to soften her stance. 'I was only joking. Of course you can come in whenever you like. It's your family's penthouse anyway.'

It wasn't long before Brett spurted out what was bothering him. 'I can't believe you've agreed to work with Chad when you're employed by me! You know the pressure I'm under at the agency.'

Millie took a deep breath. 'Have you had breakfast?'

'No.'

'Would you like some pancakes and fruit?'

Brett glanced at the half-eaten pancake on Millie's plate. 'If it's not too much trouble.'

Millie jumped up. 'I'll just pop into the kitchen and make a few more.'

Brett's eyes widened. 'You make pancakes?'

Millie tried not to smile; she got the distinct feeling that Brett didn't know his way around a kitchen. 'Of course, why don't you come inside and help me.'

Brett thought about it, then decided he didn't have much choice. He followed Millie into the kitchen. There was a knock on the door of the penthouse suite, and Brett strolled over to open it. His first thought was that Millie had been joking about pancake-making and that room service had arrived with her earlier order of a full English breakfast. Brett was disappointed when he opened the door to see Danny, who took a step backwards when he saw his brother.

Millie poked her head over Brett's shoulder. 'Danny! Do you need something from your office?'

Danny blushed. 'No. I see you're busy; I'll leave you two to it.'

Brett shut the door and rubbed his hands together. 'Come on then. Show me how to make pancakes.'

*

Danny scratched his head. Had Brett stayed in the penthouse overnight? Danny shuddered at that thought. It had been stupid of him to think of inviting Millie to tonight's *Party on the Pier*. Danny shook his head to remove the idea of having a fun time with Millie. Five thousand words were calling him, and he needed to keep focused.

*

Chad polished his shoes; this was the first time he'd done a photo shoot. Whatever his grandmother was up to was her business. He'd ask no questions, conform to her eccentricities, then get on the next plane to New York – well, the one he was already booked onto on Tuesday.

*

Brett gazed into Millie's eyes. His granny approved of her, she made the best pancakes, and he'd undervalued her for the two years she'd worked for *Miller, Casey & Harbottle*. Maybe Millie was "the one".

Millie poured Brett another coffee. 'Let's think about this. *Mosely Timmins* has an HR team who've been undertaking all the recruitment for the business. The business is expanding, and the HR team needs to offload their recruitment activities to us. The brilliant thing is we now have the capacity to help them. Why aren't you happy about this, Brett?'

Brett sighed. 'Because some of our major players won't sign their new contracts and will be leaving at the end of the month. It will take time to recruit new employees into our team.'

Millie's heart sank when she remembered Jordan living in her apartment. Would *he* be gone by the end of June? This summer was turning into a nightmare. Millie was out of her comfort zone. Why had Madame Wilhelmina "hijacked" her when she would have been of more use doing her job for Brett?

A lightbulb switched on in Millie's mind. 'When are you next meeting with Cynthia?'

'Tomorrow morning.'

'Great.'

'Why?'

'Ask her if she has any recruitment consultants to spare. They were doing their own thing before they moved over to using us. We're providing them with a whole team of recruitment specialists, and there may be one or two people in Cynthia's team who will now be out of a job.'

Brett rubbed his forehead. 'You may have a point.'

Millie held her shoulders back. 'I *do* have a point.'

Brett's green eyes twinkled, and he suppressed a desire to kiss Millie on her lips. 'I shouldn't have been so quick to hand you over to my granny. I need you more than Chad does.'

Millie's heart fluttered at the sparkle in Brett's eyes. She lowered *her* eyes as she spoke, 'Speaking of Chad, I'm meeting him at lunchtime at the beach house. He's going to take a few photos this afternoon. Goodness knows what I'm letting myself in for.'

Brett grabbed Millie's hand. 'He's only taking photographs. He'll never be able to capture the real you.'

Millie slid her hand from beneath Brett's; he was her boss! Things needed to be kept on a professional basis. 'Are you sure you can manage without me?'

Brett nodded. 'I'll have to. Anyway, I've roped in my second in command to take charge of the *Mosely Timmins* project.'

Millie gulped. She knew the answer but asked anyway, 'Who's that?'

'Jordan. He's arriving in the morning.'

17

PHOTO SHOOT

Millie dragged an overnight bag along the promenade until she reached the beach house. She lifted the bag onto the beach and rang a buzzer next to the front door. Chad opened it. He stared at the bag and flashed a white smile. 'Are you planning on staying overnight?'

Millie blushed; why were the Harbottle brothers so attractive? They were all tall, dark, and handsome with sparkling green eyes, but they were very different characters. Chad was a talented artist who travelled the world. Brett was confident and driven, although lacking attention to detail; the HR disaster sprang to mind. Danny was mean and moody on the surface, but last night he'd surprised her with his kindness. Millie could still feel his strong hand in hers, and she was suddenly curious to know why he'd come to the penthouse this morning.

Chad lifted Millie's bag off the sand. 'Let me bring this in for you. It's heavy. What have you got in there?'

Millie's thoughts returned to the present. 'Thanks, Chad. I packed a few changes of clothes for our photo shoot. I wasn't sure what to wear.' Millie caught sight of Chad's polished brown shoes, navy suit trousers and white shirt. 'Have I got the right day? You look like you're off to an important meeting.'

Chad blushed. This wasn't going to be easy; he'd nearly blown his cover by wearing the wrong clothes. What *did* photographers wear? He'd need to bluff his way through. 'I was at a meeting this morning; there's been no time to change. Good idea, though, for you to bring a selection of outfits. Let's see what you've brought with you.'

Millie unzipped the bag and was surprised when Chad pointed to the red dress she'd worn last night. 'You need to wear that dress in all the shots and bring the red hat; it's just what we need. We already have the image from last night. Today, I need to get shots of you on the beach, on a yacht, in the flower garden on the promenade, beside the lido, and on the pier. That should do it.'

Millie gasped. 'What do you mean "that should do it"? Are you planning on just one afternoon of shooting?'

Chad nodded. 'That's all I need.'

Millie felt disappointed. She thought she'd be working with Chad for longer than that. She guessed he only wanted to pay her a modelling fee for one afternoon's work. Millie looked around the gallery to establish how many models he'd used before – but she couldn't find any. Chad's paintings were of landscapes, seascapes, and famous cities. Maybe he was trying to break into painting portraits.

Millie picked up the dress. 'May I go upstairs to change?'

Chad grabbed his car keys. 'Of course, I'll go and get my car. I park it over at the hotel. Just pull the door closed behind you; it's self-locking. I'll meet you outside in fifteen minutes.'

*

Chad was standing beside a convertible BMW. He opened the door for Millie to climb in. Millie glanced up at him. 'This is nice. I wasn't expecting to be driven anywhere. It sounded like the shots you have lined up are all within walking distance of the hotel.'

Chad turned on the engine. 'Most of the shots are, except for the one on a boat. I've arranged to use a friend's yacht, but it's half an hour away down the coast. Shall we have some music?' Millie smiled, and Chad turned on the radio. He hoped the sound of music would stop Millie from asking too many questions. He needn't have worried; Millie was lost in deep deliberation.

Millie snapped out of her troubled thoughts as soon as the music stopped, and she noticed they were parked in a marina car park. Chad turned to look at her. 'Are you OK? You're very quiet.'

A tear trickled down Millie's cheek, and she wiped it away. 'I'm confused, Chad. I have no idea why your grandmother insists I spend the summer here. I'd have been more use doing my day job and helping Brett out of the mess he's in.'

'Is Brett in a mess?'

Millie nodded. 'You heard what your grandmother said last night. The recruitment business is struggling.'

'I thought that big brother Brett was invincible. Grandma always speaks highly of him.'

'Well, you're wrong. Brett's human like the rest of us; he makes mistakes.'

'What mistakes has he made?'

Millie blew her nose and forced a smile. 'Nothing. He's just had some bad luck recently. Now, which yacht are we looking for? You lead the way.'

*

Taking photographs of Millie had been more enjoyable than Chad had anticipated. She was a lovely girl. From his experience, those were few and far between. He flicked through the images on his camera. Millie was photogenic too. Chad checked the time on his phone – it was five-thirty. Right on cue, Wilhelmina walked into the beach house. 'How did it go this afternoon?'

Chad smiled. 'I got some great shots. I like Millie. She's such a genuine, natural girl.'

Wilhelmina smiled back. 'That's what I thought.'

Chad held his grandmother's gaze. 'You know she's in love with Brett?'

Wilhelmina sat down on the nearest chair. 'That wasn't supposed to happen.'

Chad poured her a glass of water. 'I don't know what you're up to, Grandma, but you can't mess with affairs of the heart.'

Wilhelmina downed the water in one. 'I need to get things back on track, and that starts with you inviting your brothers to the *Party on the Pier* tonight.'

Chad raised his eyebrows. 'What about Millie?'

'You should invite her too.'

18

PARTY ON THE PIER

Millie stood at the end of the pier and stared out to sea. Music was blaring in the background, a Ferris wheel was providing breathtaking views of the coastline, dodgem cars were creating screams and laughter, and Millie had never felt so alone. She'd only been here a week and had another eleven to go. She'd tried to find a niche for herself, but everything she'd grasped had been taken from her. Firstly, working with *Mosely Timmins* and now a modelling job that had lasted for no more than a few hours. Both times she'd been excited about filling her time, and both times she'd come down to earth with a thud.

'I got you a white wine; I thought you'd prefer it to brandy.'

Millie turned to see Danny holding out a plastic cup. 'That's very kind of you. What did you want to speak to me about this morning? I've been wondering all day what it could have been. It was nice of you to knock on a Sunday rather than just entering the penthouse. Your brother barged in this morning unannounced.' Millie pulled a face, and Danny's confidence rose.

'I was going to invite you to this.'

Millie gasped. 'The *Party on the Pier*?'

'That's right. As it happened, Chad invited all of us, so things turned out well in the end.'

Danny grinned, and Millie hugged him. 'Does that mean we're friends now?'

Chad nudged Wilhelmina. 'It looks like Millie's got a soft spot for Danny too.'

Wilhelmina sighed. 'I need to intervene.' She walked over and tapped Millie on her shoulder. 'Millie, my dear, would you mind covering for me in my hut for the next hour?'

Millie frowned. 'Your hut? What as Madame Wilhelmina? You have a hut on the pier?'

'Yes, dear, I use it occasionally.'

Impersonating Madame Wilhelmina was the last

thing Millie wanted to do, but she felt she had an obligation to help out. 'OK. Let me know where you've left your black shroud.'

*

During her time in Madame Wilhelmina's hut, Millie became confused. One woman confessed her love for Brett Harbottle and said they were "soul mates" after going to nursery together when they were two. Another said she'd been Danny Harbottle's secret girlfriend for the last two years and needed to remain a secret. And then, in contrast to an admirer of Brett, a woman said she wouldn't let him within a mile of one of her daughters. Millie struggled to give a prediction to any of them – had Wilhelmina sent them into the hut as a joke? What was she playing at? There was, however, a man who was genuinely in need of help.

Millie commenced with her opening statement: 'Please turn the sign on the door. We must not be disturbed. What do you want to know, my dear?'

The man held his head in his hands. 'I have a confession to make.'

Millie sighed. Didn't people know they should go to church to make confessions? She kept her voice low and steady, 'What would you like to confess, my dear?'

'I'm having an affair with my wife's colleague.'

Millie narrowed her eyes. 'That's very silly of you.'

'I know. I've been married to Cynthia for twenty-five years, and Greta came along at a weak moment. Those *Mosely Timmins* office parties shouldn't have free bars. Even the big boss was letting her hair down behind the marquee.'

Millie cringed, poor Cynthia. She raised an eyebrow; surely Helga Hanscombe wouldn't let her hair down at an office party? How unprofessional.

The man waved at the shrouded body. 'Hello! Is there anyone in there? Why aren't you telling me how things will turn out?'

Millie touched her forehead on top of the crystal ball. 'There will be no more contact between you and your wife's colleague. You will confess to your wife. It is unclear if she will forgive you. You will also advise your wife of Helga Hanscombe's unprofessional behaviour. That information will make your wife's life at work so much easier. You owe that to Cynthia.'

The man sat bolt upright. 'You're remarkable. How did you work out the name of Cynthia's boss?'

Millie ran her hands over the crystal ball. 'The ball tells me everything. Would you like me to tell you more about your future?'

The man jumped out of his seat. 'No thanks.

You've been very helpful.'

Millie grinned beneath her veil. 'Please turn the sign on the door before you leave.'

By the time Wilhelmina returned to relieve Millie of her duties, their relationship was fractured. Millie didn't trust the eccentric old bat. She wouldn't tell her that, but she wouldn't be used as a pawn in whatever game Wilhelmina was playing. At least with Madame Wilhelmina back in her hut, Millie could spend the rest of the evening having fun with her grandsons.

Danny was waiting outside the hut with a suggestion, 'We should go on the dodgems with Brett and Chad. We always used to go on them as boys. I'll buy the tickets while you round them up. We can share one, and I'll drive.'

Millie was thrilled with the change in Danny, which was undoubtedly fuelled by a couple of beers over the last hour while she was in shrouded confinement. It was lovely to see the brothers getting along so well. It wasn't long ago that Brett had admitted to not being close to his younger brothers. Ten years was a bit of an age gap, but not one that should matter if there was an underlying bond.

Chad jumped into the driving seat of a dodgem, and Brett climbed in next to him. Their main aim was to bump into Danny and Millie, and they met their target several times. Millie screamed, and Danny placed his left arm around her while steering the car with his right. The brothers were in fits of giggles while Millie just wished the ride was over. Her long black hair stuck out from all directions after spending an hour earlier straightening it. When their time was up, Danny helped Millie out of their car. 'OK, that was my choice. It's your turn to choose what we do next.'

Millie's legs felt like jelly, and she held onto Danny's arm as she surveyed the attractions on the pier. 'I'd like a seat near the live music while you boys go and win me a cuddly toy. You should be able to manage that between the three of you.'

Brett and Chad grinned at one another before Brett turned to Millie. 'You've set quite a target there. When we were younger, we wasted so much money trying to win cuddly toys that our parents banned us from going to fairs.'

Millie's eyes widened. 'Your parents? May I ask what happened to them?'

Danny's eyes clouded over. 'We don't have parents.'

Brett placed an arm around Danny's shoulders. 'Well, we did have parents, but not anymore. They deserted us seven years ago. They split up and went their separate ways. We don't hear from them. That's why our grandparents are so special to us.'

Millie felt a pang of guilt for her newfound dislike of Wilhelmina. Danny held his shoulders back then rubbed his hands together. 'It's Chad's turn to buy Millie a wine. I'm off to the shooting stall. The first one back with a cuddly toy gets a kiss from Millie.'

Millie threw a hand to her mouth before shouting to Danny, 'It's a deal! May the best man win.'

19

RECRUITMENT PROJECT

Five cuddly toys were propped up on the dressing table in Millie's bedroom. Danny had won three, and Brett and Chad one each. They'd all earned a kiss last night.

Millie grinned from ear to ear. Her raffle prize was becoming enjoyable. She checked the time; it was eight-forty-five. Danny would be arriving for work at nine. There was no need to avoid one another now they were friends. Brett had an appointment at *Mosely Timmins* at nine-thirty, and Chad said he had some work to do on the images from the photo shoot before he left for New York tomorrow. Millie couldn't believe that Chad was off to New York! When would he have time to do the paintings? Still, that wasn't Millie's problem. She would have an easy day today and wait for feedback from Brett about how his meeting at *Mosely Timmins* went.

*

Brett sat opposite Cynthia Althorpe. She looked drained. The bags under her eyes suggested she hadn't slept all night. He chose not to comment on her washed-out appearance. 'As I mentioned on Friday, my colleague – Jordan – will join us at ten o'clock. He's my second in command, and I'm putting him in charge of your project.'

Cynthia reached for her coffee and sipped it as she spoke, 'Have you ever been to see Madame Wilhelmina on the pier?'

Brett was taken aback. 'I can't say that I have.'

Cynthia narrowed her eyes. 'Well, she's good. Very good.'

Brett felt a tingle run down his spine. His granny popped up everywhere – what a random thing for Cynthia to say. He needed to get back on the subject of business. 'I am well aware you may have some spare employees in the HR team by outsourcing your recruitment requirements to us. If so, I could potentially make use of them in my agency.'

Cynthia's eyes bulged. She placed her coffee cup on the table. 'You can have Greta. When do you want her?'

Brett sat back in his seat. He hadn't thought Cynthia would make things so easy. 'I'll take Greta today. She can join in the meeting when Jordan arrives. It will be good to have an element of continuity between our businesses. Do you want to advise her of what's happening? I take it you won't hit any HR hurdles with the transfer. It's best to keep on the right side of employment law.'

Cynthia stood up. 'You don't need to teach Granny how to suck eggs. I'll speak to her now.'

Brett was relieved when, fifteen minutes later, Jordan walked into the meeting room. Cynthia hadn't returned yet with Greta, so he was able to fill him in on the good news. Jordan frowned. 'Do you think it's wise to accept one of Cynthia's employees without conducting a structured interview? What if Greta's not a good fit for our team? Where's Millie? I thought she'd be here today.'

Brett rubbed his forehead; Jordan had a point. 'I'm under a lot of pressure. It was Millie's idea to ask Cynthia if she had any spare staff. And, as far as Millie goes, she's off limits to us until the end of her raffle prize. Granny is putting her to use with my brother. I get the distinct feeling Millie's here to make my rich artist brother even more affluent – she was all over the place with him yesterday modelling for his next collection of work.'

Jordan's mouth fell open, and Brett continued, 'There's something I need to fill you in on; Granny announced on Saturday night that she's bought out the Miller and Casey shareholders, and we're soon to become the *Harbottle Recruitment Agency*. She also made a dig about the "recruitment business struggling". It sounds like she's focusing on the hotel; she's ploughing money into it. She's going to refurbish it and rename it the *Harbottle Harbourside Hotel.*'

Jordan raised his eyebrows. 'Wow! That's a lot of information to take in. Is there a chance we could lose our jobs?'

Brett sat back in his chair. 'We *have* to make the agency work. I thought I was more successful than my brothers until this weekend. Chad's business is taking off, and Danny's been the mastermind behind buying out Miller and Casey.' Brett smiled before continuing, 'I'm so proud of those two. I can't believe we've all drifted apart since our parents split up. I'm going to make sure that doesn't happen again.'

The meeting room door opened, and Cynthia walked in, followed by a tall, blonde bombshell. That was the best word for her – a "bombshell". Brett and Jordan's eyes were on stalks as they stood up to greet their new teammate.

A smile flickered over Cynthia's face as she officially transferred a rotten egg to Brett's team. 'Gentlemen, meet Greta. She's always up for a new challenge. She's yours from this moment on.'

Brett's green eyes twinkled as he shook hands with Greta. 'I'm Brett, and this is my second in command – Jordan. We're delighted to welcome you onboard. I'm not sure about the logistics of this as our agency is four hours away from here on the outskirts of London. You could potentially stay in Devon, and we could rent a desk for you at *Mosely Timmins*.'

Cynthia shook her head. 'That won't work. Greta should relocate. I've advised her to pack her things and leave by lunchtime.'

Jordan frowned before glancing at Brett. Brett returned Jordan's shocked expression, then composed himself before speaking, 'That's fine with us. We can offer Greta a desk at the hotel we use while we're down here.' Brett then turned his attention to Greta. 'I hope that works for you. We'll wait while you pack your things, then we can become acquainted over lunch.'

Greta flashed a smile from Brett to Jordan and then back again. 'Fabulous! I'll meet you in the foyer at noon.'

Brett had never seen such pretty eyes; they were violet in colour and enhanced beautifully by Greta's porcelain complexion and rosebud lips. What a brilliant idea of Millie's to suggest the transfer of an HR employee from *Mosely Timmins* to the new *Harbottle Recruitment Agency*. On first impression, Greta was the type of person who would make a difference. Brett's mind was working overtime about the commission package he would be offering his latest recruit. Jordan would have to watch his step; Greta could be the new Sadie.

*

It was five o'clock when Danny opened his office door. He saw Millie sitting on a sun lounger on the terrace, reading a book. It wouldn't hurt to see how she was doing. 'Living a life of luxury, I see. Good book?'

Millie lowered her sunglasses. 'Brilliant book, thank you. I found it in a pile on the coffee table. Why didn't you tell me you wrote books?'

Danny shuffled his feet. 'You didn't ask. Besides, it's just a hobby; I could never make a living out of it. Nor would I want to; I enjoy the legal and financial side of things. You could say I've got a perfect balance.'

Millie winked. 'Do you have a secret girlfriend? That would balance things out.'

Danny laughed. 'I wish! There's been no time for romance while I've been extracting Miller and Casey shareholders from our business. And now I'll be knee-deep in contracts concerning the refurbishment of the hotel.'

Millie pushed her sunglasses back up her nose. 'You work too hard.'

Danny was about to leave when he had an idea. 'Are you doing anything this evening?'

Millie sighed. 'Doesn't look like it. I've been waiting for an update from Brett on how the *Mosely Timmins* meeting went this morning. Jordan's supposed to be here too today. Neither of them has contacted me. They're having too much fun.'

Danny grinned. 'That's a shame. Fancy dinner tonight at the Beachside Bistro? They do amazing wine and seafood.'

Millie swung her legs off the sunbed. 'Count me in. What time?'

'In thirty minutes? We haven't booked, and it can get busy, even on Monday nights.'

Millie jumped up. 'It's a date! I'll meet you downstairs.'

Danny closed the door to the penthouse suite. A "date" – things were looking up!

20

TABLE FOR SIX

Danny was right; the bistro was popular. Millie was worried they wouldn't be able to squeeze a table for two in – until she saw a group of four people with two spare seats. So that's what Brett and Jordan had been up to all afternoon. They'd met an attractive blonde and roped Chad in to make a foursome. Millie frowned; she could be wrong. Maybe the blonde was Chad's date, and Brett and Danny had just stopped off for a bite to eat after a taxing day at *Mosely Timmins*. There was only one way to find out.

Millie glanced up at Danny. 'It looks like we'll be joining your brothers if they let us. Do you want to ask them, or shall I?'

Danny took the lead. 'Any chance of squeezing two hungry souls onto your table? Have you eaten already? We're famished.'

Brett's head jerked up. 'Danny! What a coincidence. Of course, you can join us. We've been here since lunchtime. We should order more food now, or we'll get thrown out for taking up a table for too long.'

Jordan glanced up at Millie. 'Hi, Millie. We missed you today at our meeting. I'm sure there's a way we can get you out of the obligations of your raffle prize. You must be bored with nothing to do all day.'

Millie was pleased to see Jordan and comforted to know that someone missed her being at work. She turned to Danny. 'This is Jordan from the agency. He's currently staying in my apartment while his new home's being renovated.'

Jordan stood up to shake Danny's hand. 'I'm pleased to meet you, Danny. I've heard a lot about you.'

Millie and Danny sat down, and Brett couldn't contain his excitement any longer. 'I took you up on your idea, Millie. This is Greta. She's now part of our team. Cynthia very kindly arranged for her to transfer to us this morning. We came here for lunch to celebrate.'

Millie's heart sank; Brett had just made another schoolboy error. He'd taken on an employee without establishing her background. Another HR failing on their boss's part. Millie wasn't surprised Cynthia was keen to offload Greta. The only trouble was Millie hadn't been at the meeting, so she couldn't raise a red flag to Brett. There was, of course, the chance that Greta was a brilliant recruitment consultant. Millie would have to sit back and wait to find out.

Danny had a question for Chad. 'What are *you* doing here?'

Chad opened his mouth, and Brett answered for him, 'I mentioned to Jordan earlier that Millie had been doing some modelling for our artist brother. When Greta advised us over lunch that she models in her spare time, Jordan suggested we introduce her to Chad.'

Millie felt Jordan's gaze boring into the side of her head. Was Jordan trying to stop her modelling for Chad? Well, he was too late. All the shots had been taken, and Millie had enjoyed doing something different for a change. Well, doing *anything* was a pleasure.

Chad smiled at Millie. 'And that's where *I* come in. I've only just got here. I had to print off the shots from yesterday. They're great, by the way. You're a natural in front of the camera, Millie. My flight to New York's early in the morning, so I'm clearing my desk before I hit the sack tonight.'

Greta's ears pricked up. 'New York?'

Brett turned to smile at her. 'Chad's a jet-setter. He came back from Cannes on Saturday. All Harbottle men are talented.'

Jordan stared at Chad. 'So, it's New York tomorrow. Where next?'

Chad placed his menu on the table while he gathered his thoughts. 'I'll be off to Madrid and Athens. I'll then fly to London for my exhibition at the beginning of August.'

Greta patted Chad's hand. 'It sounds like you're a very busy boy.'

Millie was worried about Chad's workload. 'When are you going to get time to do the paintings of me?'

Chad squeezed Millie's arm. 'Stop fretting. All plans are in place to launch *Millie's Summer Collection* on time. Trust me. I never miss a deadline.'

There was a bit too much touching going on for Jordan's liking. He tried to get Millie's attention. 'I put the rubbish bags out before I left this morning. It's going to be a hot week.'

Millie was brought back to reality. 'Good thinking. You've not been using my hairdryer, have you?'

Jordan ran a hand through his tousled blonde hair. 'Does it look like it?'

Millie chuckled. 'Good. How's the renovation work getting on at your new place?'

'It's going well. The two-seater swing has arrived, and I've bought two potted roses to train around the trellis.'

'What colour?'

'Fuchsia.'

'Perfect.'

Chad laughed. 'You two sound like an old married couple.'

Jordan blushed, and Danny raised an eyebrow. Brett couldn't take his eyes off his new recruit as he handed her a menu. 'I'd recommend the scallops or the chilli prawns.'

Greta glanced at the menu and then over at Chad. 'What would a man of the world recommend?'

Millie suppressed a snigger before noticing that Jordan and Danny were trying to keep straight faces too. Brett couldn't compete with an international artist;

he should stop trying before he made a fool of himself. How much trouble could he get into in one day?

Chad winked at Millie before responding to Greta, 'I'm going for the fish and chips.'

*

When the sun went down, the harbour came to life. The Beachside Bistro was an excellent place to people watch. Millie felt at peace. She'd had a lovely meal, half a bottle of wine, and been entertained by the charming Harbottle brothers. She was pleased Jordan was staying on the English Riviera for a week. When Jordan was there, she felt she had a connection to "home". There was only one blip on the horizon: Greta.

Chad decided to get an early night, and Brett took the opportunity to go for a short stroll on the beach. He'd been sitting down all day and needed to stretch his legs. That allowed Millie to sit next to her new colleague. 'I haven't had much chance to speak to you tonight. How long have you worked for *Mosely Timmins*?'

Greta twisted a long strand of blonde hair around her finger. 'Six weeks.'

Millie gasped. 'Six weeks!'

Jordan and Danny looked over at the girls.

Millie locked eyes with Brett's latest mistake. 'Have you worked anywhere else as a recruitment consultant?'

Greta snorted. 'What?!'

Jordan stood up at the sight of Brett returning, and he walked over to stop him in his tracks. 'You need to listen to the conversation between Millie and Greta.'

Millie's eyes narrowed. 'What job *have* you been doing in HR?'

'Administration, but I'm not very good at it. Don't tell the boys, though – that's between you and me. I find it difficult to type with my acrylics.'

Brett's colour had drained from his face, and he whispered to Jordan, 'Acrylics?'

Jordan whispered back, 'Her nails; they're fake.'

Brett rubbed his forehead. 'What are we going to do with her?'

Jordan shrugged. 'Frighten her off? Send her travelling with Chad? It's your problem, boss. I suggest you check out their credentials next time.'

The conversation had turned to whispers from Millie and face-pulling from Greta. Brett frowned at Jordan, who shook his head and held his hands in the air. Brett then glanced over at Danny, sitting alone at the end of the table. His brother was staring at Millie and Greta, who were oblivious to the fact they were being watched from all angles.

Eventually, Millie sat back in her chair and folded her arms. She stared straight ahead with a poker face. Greta turned an ugly shade of puce before pushing her chair back with a screech. She flung her fake Chanel bag over her shoulder as she stood up. Striding past Brett and Jordan, Greta spurted out her news, 'I've got better things to do than work for a deadpan business like yours. Adios mi amigos.'

Brett raised his eyebrows at Jordan. 'Was that last bit Spanish? Is she planning on going to Madrid?'

Danny's eyes shone as he congratulated Millie, 'You were amazing.' Brett and Jordan sat down, and Danny continued, 'Millie's just saved you from an HR nightmare.'

Brett stared at Millie. 'What did you say to her?'

Millie finished her wine. 'Nothing I can repeat. It was just something I heard while impersonating Madame Wilhelmina. Your grandmother must hear all sorts of things in her job.'

Brett held his hands in the air. 'How will we explain things to Cynthia?'

Millie shrugged. 'Say that Greta did a runner. Cynthia won't be surprised at all.'

Danny placed his jacket around Millie's shoulders. 'Come on; it's late. We've all got work tomorrow. You're the only one who can have a lie in.'

Millie breathed in the sea air and looked up at the stars. As far as days went, today had been a good one, a very good one indeed.

21

FREEDOM RETURNS

Brett bounded into the penthouse suite at eight-thirty in the morning. Millie was making coffee. 'Would you like one?'

Brett shook his head. 'I don't have time. I'm driving back to the office this morning. Jordan's staying down here to work on the *Mosely Timmins* project. I'm needed back at base to start rebuilding the team. I've just popped in to let you know. Anyway, I must be off. I've got a meeting scheduled for one o'clock.'

Millie was surprised Brett was so buoyant after his disaster with Greta yesterday. She didn't want to temper his good mood by reminding him not to take any shortcuts when recruiting new employees. She was sure he'd learnt a lesson. 'Good luck with that. I'll just wait here to find out what your grandmother has in store for me.'

Brett glanced over his shoulder. 'Well, you'll be waiting a while. My grandparents are off to Switzerland for an extended vacation. Granny messaged us last night. It's all right for some!'

The penthouse door closed, and Millie folded her arms. There was no way she would spend any more time in limbo. She couldn't face another day with nothing to do. Millie phoned Jordan. 'Are you going into *Mosely Timmins* today? … Great … I'm coming with you.'

*

Jordan held his car door open for Millie before closing it and rushing around to jump into the driver's seat. 'Is this wise? What would Wilhelmina and Brett say?'

Millie shrugged. 'They don't need to know.'

Jordan glanced at Millie. 'OK, you can help me, but only as a trainee recruitment consultant. You'll be of more use to me in that role. Susie and Melanie are best placed to handle the administration side of things – they're in the office and have access to the database.'

Millie let out a yelp of excitement, 'YES!!'

Jordan grinned. 'Get ready for an exciting time. I'll

teach you everything I know.'

*

Two weeks later, Brett phoned Jordan. 'I've just seen the latest report on *Mosely Timmins*. I can't believe how many candidates you've sourced for their finance roles in such a short time. I see they're already at the offer stage for nine of the twenty-five positions. Cynthia's delighted and has advised me their recruitment drive for marketing and sales roles will start soon.'

Jordan winked at a smiling Millie. 'Glad to be of service. I aim to fill all the finance vacancies within the next four weeks. I can focus on marketing and sales after that.'

An envelope on Brett's desk caught his eye. 'Oh, by the way, your new contract is here, ready for you to sign. Remind me about it when you're next in the office.'

Millie's eyes widened as she watched the smile leave Jordan's face. He finished the conversation with Brett and then glanced over at her. 'Don't ask. Things are complicated.'

*

Four weeks later, Danny was walking along the promenade when he saw Millie sitting on a wall overlooking the sea. He was pleased to see her; she'd not been lounging around in the penthouse suite for ages. He'd only bumped into her on the odd occasion when he arrived for work, but she was always rushing out. 'May I join you?'

Millie glanced up at him. 'Hello, Danny.'

'You look like you have the weight of the world on your shoulders. What have you been doing to pass the time over the last six weeks?'

Millie sighed. 'That would be telling. Why is life so complicated? Why aren't things straightforward?'

Danny put his arm around her shoulders. 'I don't like seeing you so . . . so lost.'

Millie turned to face him. 'How are *you* doing? Have you found a better work/life balance?'

Danny looked out to sea. 'I'm trying to. Something has to go for me to find the time to have a girlfriend, and I've decided what that will be.'

Millie stared out to sea too. 'What's that?'

'I'm giving up writing. My third book is finished and at the publishers. I can cross writing off my bucket list now.'

Millie frowned. 'That's a shame; I hope you don't miss it.' She thought back to the whimsical drawings in Danny's office. 'You and Chad are so talented. Have you ever thought of trying to sell *your* artwork too.'

Danny looked at Millie. '*My* artwork?'

Millie blushed. 'Oops. That's me caught out. I had a peek in your office one day; your drawings are amazing.'

Danny tried not to smile. So Millie *had* sneaked into his office when he'd left the key in the door that night. 'No, I won't be selling any artwork. My focus is now solely on my legal and finance work.'

Millie smiled at him. '*And* on trying to find a girlfriend. Would you like me to help you while I'm stuck down here on the English Riviera? I'm busy during the week now, but I'm available at weekends.

Danny couldn't help but ask, 'Isn't Jordan around at weekends?'

Millie shook her head. 'No. He works around the clock Monday to Friday, then goes home at weekends to check on the renovation work at his new place and water my pot plants.'

Danny held out his hand to shake Millie's. 'OK then – if you're sure you're up for the challenge. How are we going to do this?'

Millie reached into her bag and produced a leaflet. 'I was given this the other day. There's a singles' Country & Western night in the Bavarian Bierkeller on

Saturday.'

Danny laughed. 'A line dance in a Bierkeller?!'

Millie shrugged. 'At least anyone turning up will have a sense of humour. I'm not taking "no" for an answer. I'm your self-appointed wingwoman. Saturday night could be the start of something good.'

22

COUNTRY & WESTERN NIGHT

Millie giggled when she saw Danny in his checked shirt, jeans, Stetson, and cowboy boots. 'Why are you laughing? This is my best attempt at being a cowboy. You look amazing, by the way.'

Mille was wearing a short pink strapless ruffle dress with a wide black belt and black and pink cowboy boots. She'd complimented her outfit with a denim jacket and left her long black wavy hair loose. She grabbed Danny's hand. 'Let's have a drink in the hotel bar before we go. Make mine a beer. I don't want to be mixing drinks tonight.'

Danny's heart leapt. He'd been convinced that Millie had feelings for Jordan. What a stroke of luck the dashing recruitment consultant had to go home at weekends. It was also convenient that Chad was out of the country; he was always the one to get the girls. Danny's thoughts turned to Brett; he'd seen a twinkle in his brother's eyes when Millie was around. Well, it was time for Danny to come out of his shell. Until Millie had arrived at the penthouse, Danny hadn't realised how reclusive he'd become – he felt like a new man.

Millie held Danny's arm on the walk down the promenade. He patted her hand and whispered in her ear as they approached the Bierkeller, 'You need to let go of my arm now. It's singles night, remember? You'll spoil my chances.'

Millie extracted her hand. She was surprised she'd automatically held onto Danny. He was right, though. It would look odd if they walked in as a couple. Danny strode up to the bar and ordered two beers. He handed one to Millie. 'That's the last one I'm buying you tonight. I'm off to find a cowgirl. Which one should I go for?'

Millie glanced around. There was a lot of choice. 'How about the one with the short blonde hair and blue dress? She looks nice.'

Danny grinned. 'Good choice. I'll mosey on over and introduce myself before we do the do-si-do. Should I say, "howdy, partner"? I want to appear authentic; first impressions are important.'

Millie squirmed. 'Cut the cowboy talk, just be yourself.'

With the girl in the blue dress mesmerised by Danny, Millie wondered what she would do with herself for the rest of the evening. She should have realised that Danny would get snapped up straight away. She looked around the room to see several men looking at her; one of them was Cynthia's husband. YUCK!! Millie put her beer down on the bar and turned to make a quick exit.

'May I buy you a drink?'

Millie stood face to chest, looking up at a young, attractive cowboy with long brown hair and bright blue eyes. She turned to look at the bar. 'Well, I did have a beer, but I think someone's taken it.'

The cowboy raised his bushy eyebrows. 'You should never leave your drink unattended in a place like this. My name's Jackson. What's yours?'

'Millie, and, yes, I would like another beer, please.'

Jackson worked at the Bierkeller, but tonight was his night off. When the time came for dancing, Millie was relieved he was an expert. She followed his lead and found herself learning a new range of dance moves. She'd tried to catch sight of Danny on the dancefloor, but Jackson was swinging her around, and she had to concentrate hard to keep up.

When the time came for a break, Millie searched the room and noticed Danny in deep conversation with the woman who'd confessed her love for Brett in Madame Wilhelmina's hut. Millie was annoyed; she didn't trust that woman one bit. She was one of Wilhelmina's accomplices in making Millie look like a fool. To this day, Millie couldn't work out why Wilhelmina had played a trick on her.

The girl in the blue dress came back on the scene. She tapped the interfering woman on her shoulder before handing Danny a beer. The woman removed her Stetson, and her blonde hair fell to her shoulders. Millie raised her eyebrows – both women were fighting over Danny. Wilhelmina's accomplice fumbled in her bag before handing Danny a slip of paper and a pen. He wrote something down and handed the note back to her. She smiled at the girl in the blue dress before leaving the room.

The music started up again, and Jackson swept Millie off her feet. Danny checked the time; it was nearly eleven o'clock. He wanted to go home but couldn't leave without Millie – he needed to ensure she was safe.

By eleven-thirty, Millie had had enough. Danny watched her shake hands with her cowboy before looking over at him and pointing to the door. Danny was relieved the night was over. After saying goodbye to the girl in the blue dress, he rushed out of the room to catch up with Millie. 'Did you have a good time with your cowboy?'

Millie forced a smile. 'Yes, thanks. How did you get on with the girl in the blue dress? Why did you write a note for that woman you were talking to?'

Danny sensed Millie was jealous, and he relaxed. 'The girl in the blue dress isn't my type. The woman is the sister of the girl in the blue dress, and she asked for my phone number.'

Millie stopped in her tracks and glared at him. 'Why?!'

'Because she's had a crush on Brett since they were at nursery school. She's seen him around recently and hopes to bump into him when he's next down here. She wants to send me her contact details so I can let her know when he returns.'

Millie frowned. 'Surely you didn't give her your number?'

'Of course not. I missed a digit off.'

Millie slipped her arm through Danny's. 'That woman came into Madame Wilhelmina's hut when I was covering for her. Do you think she's worked out that Wilhelmina's Brett's grandmother?'

Danny raised his eyebrows. 'I hope not. Brett would be devastated!'

Millie nudged Danny in his ribs before frowning. 'I thought Wilhelmina had sent her into the hut as a joke to make me look like a fool. There were two other women I thought were fake too.'

'Why? What did *they* say?'

Millie blushed before responding, 'One said she wouldn't let her daughters anywhere near Brett, and the other said she'd been your secret girlfriend for two years and wanted to remain secret.'

Danny turned Millie to face him before holding her shoulders. 'I have a confession to make.' Millie's face dropped. 'Chad told me our grandmother is against you falling for Brett or me, so she sent you in the hut to put a spanner in the works.'

Millie was fuming. 'Why would she be against me joining the family?'

Danny gulped. 'Have you thought of doing that?'

Millie shook her head. 'Of course not, don't be silly. I just want to know what your grandmother has against me when she's gone to so much trouble to hijack me this summer.' Millie shrugged free from Danny's grasp. 'To be honest, I'm fed up with all of this.'

Danny didn't know what to say. He was no wiser than Millie with what his grandmother was up to. 'I apologise for my family, Millie. I'll walk you back to the penthouse.'

*

Millie unlocked the penthouse door to the sight of a gold envelope on the floor. She stared at Danny. 'I wonder what this is?'

Danny looked over her shoulder as she opened the envelope to reveal an invitation:

> *You are cordially invited to attend the launch party for:*
>
> ## Millie's Summer Collection
>
> *On Saturday 1st August at 7.00 p.m.*
>
> **Venue:** Chad Harbottle Gallery, London

Millie was shocked; the 1st of August was next week. 'I'd forgotten about Chad doing the paintings. I've been so busy working for Jordan.'

Danny frowned. 'You're working for Jordan? I thought you worked for Brett?'

Millie sighed. 'It's a long story. I just want to curl up and cry.'

Danny cupped Millie's sad face in his hands. 'Don't cry.'

Millie stared into Danny's deep green eyes before she felt the softness of his lips on her forehead. 'If I curl up with you tonight, will you promise not to cry?'

Millie nodded before closing the penthouse door.

23

MILLIE'S SUMMER COLLECTION

Danny had a secret girlfriend. Her name was Millie, and they'd been together for a week. They knew Wilhelmina would disapprove of their relationship. So, for the foreseeable future, Danny and Millie decided to keep it under wraps.

Tonight was going to be their biggest challenge; they were in London for the launch of *Millie's Summer Collection*. Wilhelmina and her husband, Wilfred, had flown in from Switzerland that morning. Millie was excited about seeing the paintings but less keen to see Wilhelmina. The last seven weeks had passed by in a flash. Millie had been busy working with Jordan, and now she had the added distraction of Danny. With Wilhelmina back in the country, Millie's secret life was at risk.

Danny held the door of the *Chad Harbottle Gallery*

open for Millie to enter. Brett was already inside talking to Chad. They turned to greet the model and their brother. Chad lifted two glasses of champagne off a tray and handed them to the VIP guests. He flashed his trademark white smile at Millie. 'It's great to see you. You must be excited to see the results of our afternoon together on the English Riviera.'

Millie smiled back. 'Yes, I am. I can't believe you met your deadline.' Millie stared at the six easels in the middle of the room shrouded in red velvet. Several guests had already arrived and were wandering around, champagne glasses in hand, as they viewed Chad's other work.

Danny noticed a few "SOLD" signs on some of Chad's paintings. 'Looks like business is good this evening. The paintings of Millie will be a total sell-out, I'm sure of that.' Danny squeezed Millie around her waist, and she stepped aside when Brett gave them a funny look. They needed to keep their relationship secret until they had the family's approval.

Several more guests arrived, followed by Wilhelmina, who signalled to a staff member for help. A ramp was quickly erected outside for Wilfred to enter the gallery on a mobility scooter. Brett and Danny stood open-mouthed as Chad went over to kiss his grandmother and shake his grandfather's hand. Brett and Danny followed at a pace and stood in front of their grandfather. 'Why are you driving that?'

Wilhelmina tutted. 'Wilfred wasn't happy about bringing it tonight, but I've been keeping an eye on him. He shouldn't overdo it so soon after a hip replacement operation. I took your grandfather to Switzerland to convalesce; I'm not having him mess up our chances of retaining our salsa title next year.'

Wilfred hopped off his scooter and went over to kiss Millie's hand. She was shocked. 'So you're the model the whole family's been talking about.'

Millie blushed. 'I wouldn't go that far, but I did pose for a few photographs for Chad.'

Chad clinked his glass with a knife, and the guests fell silent. 'I would like to thank you all for coming here this evening. I recognise many of you, but I can also see some new faces who have come to view my work. Your support humbles me.' There were smiles throughout the crowd, and a few clapping hands before Chad continued, 'Tonight, I have the greatest pleasure to unveil *Millie's Summer Collection*, which was inspired one afternoon on the English Riviera.'

There were gasps around the room as the lights in the gallery dimmed, and spotlights lit up the easels. Six staff members pulled at the red velvet covers to reveal a collection of whimsical paintings. Millie squinted. She couldn't see her face. The images were either rear view or with just a hint of a profile showing from beneath her hat. Millie stared at Danny; was he the artist? The paintings were in the same style as the ones in his office.

Chad took time for his audience to recover from the shock before continuing, 'I am sure you will agree with me that this work is exceptional. It's whimsical, magical and like nothing that's out there today. Unfortunately, I didn't paint these masterpieces; my grandfather did.'

Chad held out his arm to identify a smiling Wilfred to the crowd. When the audience had adjusted to the surprise, they clapped wholeheartedly. Whistles and cheers bounced off the gallery walls as Wilfred took a bow.

Millie felt numb. As the "faceless" model, she withdrew to the back of the crowd of art critics who were now jostling for positions at the front. Cameras flashed as Wilfred posed next to his paintings. Members of the press were keen to interview Chad regarding his grandfather's hidden talent, while staff at the gallery were taking details of potential commissions for both artists. Millie glanced over at Brett and Danny having a brotherly chat before narrowing her eyes and staring at Wilhelmina, who sensed Millie's agitation.

Wilhelmina grabbed her husband's arm. 'You should get back on your scooter. You've had your moment of glory; let's return to our hotel.' Wilhelmina waved at Chad. 'Round the family up as soon as you've finished. We'll have a drink at the hotel to celebrate.'

Chad walked over to Millie. 'I apologise for being less than truthful with you, but what my grandmother wants, she gets.'

Millie raised her eyes to the ceiling. 'I've heard *that* before.'

Brett was amazed by their grandfather's hidden talent; Danny wasn't surprised at all. 'I have a selection of Grandpa's artwork in my office. Grandma asked me to try to sell it to give him a boost. I've been too busy with everything else to look into it.'

Brett winked at his brother. 'Give the whole lot to Chad; you've already got enough on your plate. Chad seems happy to share his gallery. Our grandfather's a superstar after tonight.'

Danny high-fived Brett before picking up a couple of spare glasses of champagne and handing one to his brother. It felt good to have a bond again with Brett. Danny hadn't realised how much he'd missed it.

*

Danny had been right; *Millie's Summer Collection* was a sell-out. It helped that Wilfred's work wasn't as expensive as Chad's, but all-in-all the reviews of the paintings were exceptional. It was refreshing to have a new artist on the scene.

The family were back at their London hotel by ten o'clock. Millie made a bee-line for Wilhelmina. 'I'm not happy with you. You've hijacked me for the summer when Brett needs me in a crisis; you tried to make a fool of me by sending in fake clients to your hut on the pier, and, by the way, I know why you did that.'

Wilhelmina raised her eyebrows. 'Why did I do that?'

'Because you don't want me to be part of your family. I'm not stupid. Someone tried to put me off Danny by saying she was his secret girlfriend. Someone else said they wouldn't let their daughters go near Brett. Then there's this woman who keeps turning up saying she's been in love with Brett since nursery school. I've lost all trust in you.'

Wilhelmina sipped her sherry. 'Go on; I must have done more wrong than that.'

Millie channelled her thoughts. 'You have. By making me think Chad was doing the paintings and that we would have fun over the summer. Honestly, Wilhelmina, I have no idea why you sent me to the English Riviera in the first place.'

Wilhelmina placed her glass on a table. 'Let me tell you.'

Millie's eyes widened as she waited for Wilhelmina's confession. 'When I met you at the fair at

Easter, I knew you were a decent person. It was very convenient you worked with Brett, who is not good at his job. So an insider from the recruitment agency has been useful. Chad has also informed me that Brett's in a mess.'

Millie gulped, and Wilhelmina held up her hand to stop her from speaking. 'It's been challenging for me since the boys' parents left. It's my job to keep the family together, and as hard as I tried, I couldn't do that. That's where you came in. You've been the glue to repair our bond. It pained me to see Danny becoming a recluse, so I thank you for bringing him out of his shell. Your job with Danny is done; he doesn't feature in your future – none of my grandsons do.'

Millie's heart sank. 'But I like Danny.'

Wilhelmina waved a hand in the air. 'Like is not enough.'

Millie lowered her eyes. 'I have no idea what to do now.'

Wilhelmina patted Millie's arm. 'There's no need to worry, my dear. All will become clear in the coming weeks.'

24

TIME TO REFLECT

Millie sat on the train with Danny on their way back to Devon. 'Have you ever thought about buying a car?'

Danny shrugged his shoulders. 'Why do I need a car? I live and work at the hotel.'

Millie glanced sideways at him. 'Have you ever thought of buying a house?'

Danny raised his eyebrows. 'Why do I need a house when I have a hotel at my disposal?'

Millie cringed. Wilhelmina had been right; Danny wasn't the one for her. She needed to break off with him sooner rather than later, but that would be awkward when she still had another month left in the penthouse. There was only one thing for it; she had to get Danny to lose interest in *her*.

*

It was the beginning of August, and with the school holidays in full swing, the hotel was busier than usual. Millie stood on the terrace of the penthouse suite and tutted at the sight of cars parked on double yellow lines. Traffic wardens were constantly issuing tickets when people couldn't bother to park in the hotel car park to offload their cases. Why did they want to jump out of their cars at the front door? Millie counted four illegally parked cars and one camper van. A camper van?! Millie rushed out of the penthouse and headed for the lift.

There was a green snake on the camper van's passenger seat, and Millie waited until the driver returned. 'Hello Zane, long time, no see. I thought you were spending the summer further down the coast.'

Zane took a step back at the sight of Millie leaning against his van. 'Hi, Millie. I'm back for a few days. I need to cover for a stall holder on the market.'

Millie looked up and down the promenade. 'We can't talk here, there are traffic wardens. I need to ask you a favour.'

Zane's eyes twinkled beneath his sunglasses. 'Jump in then, darling. We can park up in my usual place.'

*

At seven o'clock, Millie's phone buzzed with a message from Danny:

Hi, Millie. I can't make it tonight. An old friend's turned up and needs me to help him out. I'll see you in the morning when I arrive for work. Danny X

Millie let out a sigh of relief. That was the end of her brief fling with Danny. If he didn't dump *her*, she could end things with *him* for not revealing he was going on a double date with Zane tonight. Danny was so immature.

*

The following morning, Millie waited for Danny to arrive for work. As anticipated, Danny looked dishevelled and racked with guilt. Millie chose to make it easy for him. 'I don't want to be in a relationship anymore. We can still be friends, but we're too young to settle down like a boring married couple. If nothing else, your grandmother will be delighted. Do you agree?'

Danny managed a weak smile. 'Did you see me out last night with Zane and those two girls? I can't believe that Zane knows Poppy.'

Millie frowned. 'Poppy?'

'The girl in the blue dress from the Bierkeller. I

didn't think she was my type, but we have a lot in common. I'm sorry if I've hurt you, Millie.'

Millie felt a weight lifting from her shoulders. She grabbed her bag. 'I'm not hurt, Danny, don't you worry about that. I must rush now, or I'll be late for work with Jordan.'

Danny held the penthouse door open for her. 'When will you tell Brett you're working for Jordan?'

Millie smiled. 'I won't. I've only got a month left, then my life will return to normal. I'll be back working in the office and sharing my apartment with Jordan.'

Danny frowned. 'I thought you said Jordan was only staying at yours for three months while his place was renovated. When you get back, the three months will be up. You've done well getting him to pay the rent while you've been away – he's been away, too.' Millie hadn't thought of that. Her stomach sank; she'd need to advertise for a new flatmate as soon as she got home.

*

Jordan was on the phone when Millie entered their office. He waved to her and smiled when she bent down to smell the vase of flowers on her desk. As soon as his call ended, he sat back in his chair. 'Do you like the flowers? They're from my garden back home. Let me get you a coffee, and then you can tell me all about Saturday night.'

Millie was in a daze; the exhibition seemed a lifetime ago. First, she'd had the shock about Wilfred being the artist, then the awkward discussion with Wilhelmina, followed by colluding with Zane yesterday, which resulted in Danny now being in the arms of Poppy. Jordan handed her a coffee, and she summarised the chain of events.

Jordan took a deep breath. 'Wow! You've had an eventful weekend. I spent mine clearing out a section of my garden.'

Millie looked over the rim of her coffee cup. 'Are you disappointed in me for having a brief fling with Danny?'

Jordan lowered his eyes. 'I can't say I'm surprised. You've had three Harbottle brothers from which to choose. What else were you supposed to do while you're down here at weekends? You wouldn't have gone for Danny in the real world.' Jordan raised his eyes to stare at her. 'Brett's more your type.'

Millie was relieved Jordan was making light of her foolishness. She let out a chuckle. 'Well, as far as Madame Wilhelmina's concerned, none of her grandsons feature in my future.'

A light switched on behind Jordan's eyes. 'I'm pleased to hear that.'

Millie finished her coffee. 'Anyway, what's

happening with you? Will you tell me why you won't sign your new contract?'

Jordan sighed. 'I like Brett, but he's not in the right job. While he's at the head of the agency, we're effectively on a sinking ship. I can't afford for that to happen to me; my new mortgage is huge. I've been putting the feelers out and now have two job offers to choose from.'

Millie gasped. 'But what will *I* do if the agency closes? I need to pay my rent.'

Jordan sat forward in his chair and tried to offer reassurance. 'Why do you think I've been training you up as a recruitment consultant? You're good, Millie. Really good. You'll have more options now when the company fails.'

Wilhelmina had heard enough, and she tiptoed away from the part-open door. She knew she needed to return to Devon sooner rather than later. With all the jigsaw pieces now to hand, Wilhelmina could put them in place.

25

WHEN A PLAN COMES TOGETHER

Two days later, a grand piano was wheeled into the bar at the soon-to-be-renamed *Harbottle Harbourside Hotel*. Danny scratched his head as he sat on a barstool next to Poppy. What on earth was his grandmother up to now? Poppy squeezed Danny's hand. 'I'm so excited Daisy and Brett will meet up again tonight. They haven't seen each other for so long.'

Danny sipped his beer. He hoped Brett would recognise Daisy; she'd indeed recognised *him* back in June. 'I think we should have given Brett the heads up that Daisy's joining us later.'

Poppy's eyes sparkled. 'Definitely not! That would spoil the excitement.'

Danny wondered *who* it would spoil the excitement for; he guessed it would be Poppy. He wasn't comfortable about this at all. He wished he hadn't told his new girlfriend that Brett had been summoned to the hotel for an important meeting with their grandmother this afternoon. Danny glanced at the time on the clock behind the bar. That meeting had been going on for two hours – what could they be talking about?

No one was more surprised than Danny when, twenty minutes later, Brett walked into the bar, sat down at the piano, and began to play. Wilhelmina prodded her youngest grandson on his shoulder. 'You won't remember Brett attending piano lessons when he was small. He carried on for quite a few years. It was a shame your parents couldn't afford to buy a piano at the time. Brett would have been a concert pianist by now.'

Danny's eyes were on stalks. 'So, *you've* bought him a piano now? When's he going to get time to use it?'

Wilhelmina winked before heading off to see Jordan. She knocked on his office door. 'Working late again, I see.'

Jordan smiled before straining his ears. 'Afraid so, is there live music in the bar tonight?'

Wilhelmina waved a hand in the air. 'Oh, it's only

Brett on the piano.'

Jordan jumped out of his chair. 'This I *must* see!'

Wilhelmina closed the office door. 'I'm sure Brett will be playing for a while; he's got a lot of missing time to catch up on. Brett's at his happiest when he's lost in his music.'

Wilhelmina signalled for Jordan to sit down. She then sat opposite him. 'Brett no longer works for the *Harbottle Recruitment Agency*. He's now the ambassador of this hotel. That suits him much better. Brett's not good with the detail of things, but he's charming and musical, and he'll bring the type of clientele through our doors who can afford to pay to stay here once we've undergone our refurbishment.'

Jordan's mouth fell open, and Wilhelmina continued, 'That leaves me with a vacancy for the Head of the recruitment business. I want to offer that position to you.' Jordan reached for a glass of water. What was happening here? Was he in a dream?

Wilhelmina tapped her fingers on Jordan's desk. 'Well – are you going to accept my offer?'

Jordan stood up and held out his hand to shake Wilhelmina's. 'Yes, thank you. It's what I've always wanted.'

Wilhelmina glanced over her shoulder as she left

the room. 'Oh, and don't spend too much time training Millie to become a recruitment consultant. That's not what she's destined to do.'

Once Jordan had composed himself, he phoned Millie. 'You need to come down to the bar. You'll never believe what's going on. I'll buy a bottle of champagne and see you in ten minutes.'

Jordan bought the champagne and nodded to Danny and Poppy before finding a table for two next to a window overlooking the sea. Millie breezed through the bar to join him. 'Since when did the bar have a grand piano?'

Jordan handed her a glass of champagne. 'Take a big sip – I have lots to tell you. Jordan advised Millie of his and Brett's new roles but omitted to mention what Wilhelmina had said about Millie's future. As far as Jordan was concerned, Millie would be working with him at the agency.'

Millie took another big sip of her drink. 'I'm thrilled for you, Jordan. I'm pleased for Brett too. I can't believe that's him over there playing the piano! Whoever would have guessed?'

The piano playing stopped to cheers and whistles, and a smiling Brett took a bow before walking over to join Jordan and Millie. Jordan stood up and reached for a chair for his former boss. 'Take a seat. I'll pop up to the bar to get another glass.'

Millie grinned from ear to ear. 'You're so talented, Brett. Are you happy with your new role?'

Brett held a hand to his chest. 'It's what I've always wanted. I'm so relieved. I can't believe Granny's done this. A tremendous weight's been lifted from me. I plan to make this hotel the best on the English Riviera.'

Jordan poured a drink for Brett and topped Millie's glass up. He held his glass out. 'Here's to you, Brett, I wish you every success in your new role.'

Brett clinked glasses with Jordan. 'You'll be successful in my old role; I know it. Granny always knows what's best.'

Millie let out a gasp. 'It's that annoying woman!'

Brett and Jordan turned to see a blonde-haired woman talking to Danny and Poppy. Brett blushed. 'Well, I never. That's Daisy; we used to go to nursery school together, and every other school after that. She's got an amazing singing voice. I'm sure that's her sister, Poppy, with her hand on Danny's leg. What's *she* doing here?'

Brett turned to face Millie. 'Why's Daisy annoying?'

Millie blushed. 'I've done it again. I've got hold of the wrong end of the stick. That woman – Daisy –

came into Madame Wilhelmina's hut when I was covering for her on the pier.'

Brett stared at Millie. 'And?'

'Daisy said she was in love with you and had been since you were two.'

'Didn't she get married?'

'I didn't ask.'

Brett didn't take his eyes off Daisy as he sipped his champagne. When he'd finished the last drop, he stood up. 'Excuse me, you two. I have unfinished business.'

Jordan could sense Millie's embarrassment. 'You've certainly stirred things up since you've been down here.' Millie held her hands over her eyes, and Jordan continued, 'For the better, I might add.'

Millie lowered her hands. 'Madame Wilhelmina knows what she's doing. I've been a pawn in her game, and now I'm redundant.'

Jordan reached out to hold Millie's hand, then decided against it. Things were different now that he was her boss. 'You're not redundant as far as I'm concerned. You'll always be part of my team.'

Millie's eyes clouded over. 'But it won't be the same, though, will it? How can I complain about the boss to Susie and Melanie when the boss is *you*?'

Jordan managed a small laugh. Millie was right; things would never be the same again.

26

SECONDMENT ACCOMPLISHED

At two o'clock on the 31st of August, Jordan opened the door of his Porsche for Millie to climb inside. 'Come along. It's time to go home.'

There was no fanfare or anyone to wave her off. Millie had completed her raffle prize and left as quietly as she'd arrived. She felt deflated; Jordan sensed her disappointment. 'It's been quite a summer, Millie. We've both been working far too hard. I've let the team in the office know we won't be returning until Monday. As soon as we get back, I'll move my things out of your apartment so you can find a new flatmate. We need time to recalibrate before we take on the challenge of rebuilding the business.'

Millie glanced sideways at her boss. 'Will you be

signing your contract?'

Jordan smiled. 'The one for my new role – yes.'

*

The four-hour journey seemed much longer; when Jordan opened the car door for Millie to step out just before six o'clock, she felt fatigued. 'I'll drop off my case before I pop to the shop to get some bread and milk.'

Jordan's heart sank. He'd spent so much time with Millie over the summer that he'd miss her. 'I need bread and milk too. I'll wait for you to drop your case off and drive you to the supermarket. I need to pick up a ready meal for tonight.'

Millie smiled. 'That would be great, I've got a few ready meals in the freezer, so I'm sorted for dinner.'

Millie came out of her apartment in tears. 'The electricity's gone off. I've lost a freezer-full of food, and the kitchen's flooded.'

Jordan jumped out of his car and threw his arms around her. 'There's nothing we can't fix together. Let me have a look at the damage.'

It was obvious Millie couldn't live in an apartment without electricity; Jordan insisted he return the favour of temporary accommodation.

At the supermarket, Jordan grabbed a trolley. 'We may as well stock up for the week, then we can enjoy our few days off. You won't be searching for a new flatmate for a while.'

Millie felt comforted by that thought. 'What ready meals should we buy for tonight?'

Jordan winked. 'I'll cook for us; just leave that to me. It's more fun cooking for two than one. There'll be no more ready meals while you're living at mine.'

*

The electric gates of Jordan's property opened, and he drove down the drive pointing out to Millie the work he'd undertaken in the garden during the summer. 'So that's where you got the flowers from. They had a beautiful perfume. We should pick some to have in the house; that's if you don't mind.'

Jordan grinned. 'Pick as many as you like. The more you pick, the more they'll grow.'

Jordan unlocked the door to his home and picked up a scrap of paper off the mat. 'It's a note from one of the builders about a delivery. They've locked it in the garage. I wonder what it could be?'

Millie smiled. 'Don't ask me. Let's go and have a look.'

Jordan opened the garage door to the sight of a

large wooden crate. Jordan's face dropped, and Millie frowned. 'Why does it say: *Chad Harbottle Gallery* on the side of that box?'

Jordan's first thought had been to close the garage door, but Millie had been eagle-eyed to notice the signage on the crate. Jordan sighed; Millie would find out one day – he may as well confess to her now, 'Because *I* bought *Millie's Summer Collection*.'

Millie threw a hand to her mouth. 'But you weren't at the exhibition.'

'I put a call into Chad, and he reserved the paintings for me.'

'Have you seen them?'

'No. But, from what you've told me, I may have made a rash decision. Not one of them shows your face.'

Millie burst out laughing. 'Well, you got lucky there! What are you going to do with them?'

Jordan blushed. 'Hang them on the wall in the hall.'

Millie frowned. 'Well, you need to look at them first, but I think they'd look better on the first floor landing. Thank goodness none of them looks like me!'

Jordan's grey eyes twinkled. 'If they don't look like

you I'll send them back.'

Millie giggled, and Jordan couldn't help himself. He stepped forward and took her into his arms before kissing her. Millie's knees went weak, and she clung to him. Jordan stroked her hair as he held her close. 'This isn't going to work. I can't be your boss, so I'm firing you now.'

Millie couldn't care less if she was hired or fired. She just wanted another kiss. She glanced up at this incredible man. 'How will I pay my rent?'

'You won't need to pay rent if you live with me.'

'But what will I do with myself?'

Jordan kissed her again. 'I can think of plenty of things, but you won't be one of my recruitment consultants. Madame Wilhelmina has predicted that.'

Millie held her head against Jordan's chest. 'I feel bad. You've been paying my rent all summer, and you hardly ever stayed in my apartment.'

Jordan squirmed. 'Now *I* feel bad. I didn't pay your rent. Brett said *he* would do it.'

Millie turned to face Jordan. 'Do you think Brett remembered to pay the rent?'

The realisation hit Jordan, and he punched the air. 'No!! What a stroke of luck!'

Millie's shoulders slumped. 'Now I'm jobless *and* homeless.'

Jordan sensed Millie's concern, and his brain clicked into action. 'I know of a job that would be ideal for you.'

'What's that?'

'Executive Assistant to the HR Director at *Mosely Timmins*.'

'Working for Cynthia? Won't that be based in Devon?'

'It's home-based. Cynthia will travel a lot with the business expansion; she'll be in London more than Devon.'

'Do you think I'd get it?'

'It's worth a try.'

27

A FRESH START

On Monday the 7th of September, Millie had a new job. Cynthia was travelling from Devon to the offices of the *Harbottle Recruitment Agency*. She was bringing Millie's equipment to enable her to work from home. Millie was nervous about going into the office. She turned to Jordan as they drove into the car park. 'What will Susie and Melanie say about all of this?'

Jordan turned off the ignition. 'I'm sure they'll be pleased for you.'

Jordan strode into the office to a round of applause and shouts of, 'Welcome back, Boss!'. Jordan smiled as he headed for Brett's office, and Millie walked over to her old desk, which was occupied by the temp who'd been doing her job over the summer. She felt out of place. What would she do for the next hour until

Cynthia got there?

Millie needn't have worried; Susie produced a bouquet, a box of chocolates, and a leaving card. 'These are for you. We knew you wouldn't want a fuss, but we wanted to do something.'

Millie hugged her friend. 'I'll still be popping into the office occasionally. Jordan's said Cynthia can use the boardroom for meetings when she's in London.'

Melanie looked over Millie's shoulder, the main office had emptied. There was just the temp still sitting at his desk. 'Talking of the boardroom, we should go in there now.' She took hold of Millie's arm and guided her into the room to cheers from Millie's former colleagues. Pastries and cakes were displayed on the table, along with a fruit basket and jugs of orange and apple juice.

Jordan raised his hands in the air. 'Don't look at me; it's the team's idea. They wanted to give you a send-off.'

Susie handed Millie a plate and a glass of orange juice before declaring the impromptu buffet open. 'Tuck in, everyone. Millie and Jordan have less than an hour to update us on their summer on the English Riviera. What have you been doing with yourselves? Apart from winning the *Mosely Timmins* contract and allowing them to poach Millie?'

Jordan bit into a Chelsea bun before wiping his mouth on a serviette. 'We couldn't possibly tell you everything in less than an hour. Millie was great with winning the *Mosely Timmins* contract. It couldn't have come at a better time for us. She's also been doing some modelling work.'

There were gasps around the room, and Millie choked on her apple turnover before setting things straight. 'That wasn't as glamorous as it sounds. Jordan's been working around the clock to keep *Mosely Timmins* happy, and I've done my best to help. The worst part was the first week when I had nothing to do. I must say, a highlight for me was seeing Brett playing the piano.'

Melanie scoffed. 'Brett plays the piano?!'

Millie nodded. 'Very well, I might add. I'm hoping we'll all get discounted rates at the *Harbottle Harbourside Hotel* once it's been refurbished. Brett plans to turn it into the best hotel on the English Riviera. He'll be a brilliant ambassador for it.' There were impressed nods and raised eyebrows all round.

Jordan had been right; an hour wasn't long enough to relay the experiences of a whole summer. Millie was surprised by the time when the temp opened the boardroom door and exclaimed, 'Cynthia Althorpe from *Mosely Timmins* is here.'

Jordan glanced around at the mess; there were crumbs on the floor and screwed-up serviettes on paper plates. He darted out of the room to greet Millie's new boss. 'Cynthia! It's great to see you. What time did you set off this morning? How was the traffic?'

'I left at six, and the traffic was fine.' The pair shook hands, and Cynthia smiled at the new Head of the *Harbottle Recruitment Agency*. 'Congratulations on your promotion!'

Jordan blushed. 'Thank you, it was quite unexpected but a nice surprise.'

Cynthia lowered her voice. 'Are you sure you want to lose Millie? I was shocked when she applied for my vacancy.'

Jordan guided Cynthia into his office. 'Of course, I don't want to lose Millie, but she's ready for a change, and who am I to stand in her way?' Jordan pulled out a chair for Cynthia. 'You can use my office this morning. The boardroom's in a bit of a mess. The team wanted to have a send-off for Millie.'

Cynthia rummaged through her bag. 'That's fine with me. I just need to hand over Millie's equipment and a parcel for her that arrived at the office on Friday.'

'A parcel for Millie was delivered to your office on Friday?'

'That's right. It surprised me too. It came soon after I offered Millie the job.'

Cynthia pulled her car keys out of her bag. 'There, found them! You wouldn't mind asking someone to get the parcel out of my boot, would you? There's also a laptop, printer, and phone on the passenger seat. If they could be brought in too, that would be great. I can't stay for longer than forty-five minutes as I'm on my way to the airport.'

Jordan took hold of the keys. 'Of course, that's no problem at all. Would you like a drink?'

Cynthia was already head down, scribbling on a notepad. 'Cappuccino, please. Then send in Millie.'

While Millie was in discussion with her new boss, Jordan went to collect the items from Cynthia's car. He was impressed that Millie was being given brand new, top-of-the-range equipment to do her job. It meant that *Mosely Timmins* wasn't short of cash. Executive Assistant to the HR Director was a new role too. Jordan was surprised Helga Hanscombe was being so accommodating to Cynthia. Millie had described Helga as a "Rottweiler".

It took two trips to carry Millie's equipment into the office. Jordan then went back and opened the car boot. He was shocked to see such a large package; Cynthia had folded her back seats down to make room for it. Jordan went to lift it; the package was heavy too. What on earth had arrived at *Mosely Timmins* for Millie? Jordan carried the package into the now tidy boardroom and checked the clock on the wall; Cynthia would be leaving soon. He'd run Millie home with her equipment before lunch so they could both get on with their new jobs.

The door to Jordan's office opened, and Cynthia walked out. 'Oh, there you are. Have you got my keys?'

Jordan handed them over. 'Now, I meant what I said. Any time you're in this area and need a meeting room, you can use ours free of charge.'

Cynthia turned as she exited the building. 'Thanks. I'll take you up on that.'

28

WHAT'S IN THE PACKAGE?

As soon as Cynthia left, the temp handed Jordan a message. 'What?! Why didn't you tell me sooner?' The temp hung his head, and Jordan composed himself. 'Don't worry, at least my office is available now.'

Jordan went to speak to Millie, 'I was going to drive you home with your equipment, but *Ennis Everglades* are coming in at eleven o'clock. I've got ten minutes to prepare.'

Millie smiled. 'Don't worry; I'm sure Susie or Melanie won't mind giving me a lift in their lunch break. You do what you need to, and I'll see you at home tonight.'

Jordan went to kiss her but decided not to in front of the staff. He pointed to Millie's equipment in the corner of the room. 'There's your laptop, printer, and phone. There's also a large parcel in the boardroom that arrived for you at *Mosely Timmins* on Friday. Cynthia kindly brought it with her today. I must dash now. See you later.'

Millie was intrigued. She went straight into the boardroom. She tried to move the package but couldn't lift it on her own. She noticed two chauffeur-driven cars pull into the car park, and six members of *Ennis Everglades* climb out. Jordan wouldn't fit them all in his office; he'd need to use the boardroom. Millie called to Susie, 'Can you help me shift this?'

Susie sensed the urgency and ran over to help Millie shove the parcel into the main office. However, they hadn't accounted for the outer covering being worn away by the friction against the carpet tiles. By the time they'd moved it to the far side of the office, part of the wrapping had peeled away.

Jordan strode through the office and held the main door open for his visitors. 'This is a nice surprise. Please come into the boardroom, and I'll arrange for drinks.'

The visitors all turned to look at Millie, standing in front of the part-covered package. She recognised most of them – they'd been major clients until they pulled the plug on their contract at the start of the summer. The Operations Director pointed to the parcel. 'What have you got there?'

Millie's heart was thumping, she'd only seen the bottom eighteen inches of the five-foot-high package, but she'd guessed what it was. Melanie couldn't believe that Millie was being so rude. Why wasn't she answering such an important person? She walked over to the parcel and ripped the rest of the covering off.

There were gasps throughout the office, and the Chief Executive of *Ennis Everglades* stepped forward to take a better look. He put his glasses on to scrutinise the portrait of Millie. 'Is this a Chad Harbottle? I'm a big fan of his work. I had no idea he painted portraits.' He turned to look at Millie, then back at the painting. 'It's an excellent likeness.'

Susie noticed Jordan's shocked expression and Millie's awkwardness. She stood in front of the visitors with a pad and pen. 'Why don't I take your drinks order? Melanie will give me a hand in getting them. You've chosen the right day to visit. We've got cakes over from Millie's leaving party.'

The Chief Executive stared at Jordan. 'Millie's leaving?'

Jordan nodded. 'I'm afraid so. Millie's taken on a role at *Mosely Timmins* from today. We'll still be in contact, though, as she'll be working for one of our major clients.'

The Operations Director raised her eyebrows. 'You're providing a service for *Mosely Timmins*? They're expanding into Europe. That's lucrative business for you.'

Jordan smiled. 'It certainly is. Now, let's move into the boardroom, and you can tell me what I can do for *you*.'

The Chief Executive stared at Jordan with admiration. 'If you can afford to commission a Chad Harbottle painting of Millie for her leaving present, then your business must be doing well. I know he's Brett's brother – but he doesn't do anything for free *or* at a discount.'

With Jordan and his visitors engrossed in their meeting, the rest of the staff in the office huddled around Millie's portrait. She hadn't seen Chad capture an image of her on the night they were all at the Beachside Bistro. She was wearing her white broderie anglaise dress, and her long, black, wavy hair was blowing slightly in the breeze. There was a beautiful pink sunset behind her, and the colour of the sea brought out the cornflower blue of her eyes. An envelope was attached to the package, and Millie went into Jordan's office to open it in private.

There was a white card inside with gold embossed lettering on the front, which read:

THANK YOU

Millie opened the card and read the message from Wilhelmina:

Dear Millie

It gives me great pleasure to send you Chad's first portrait as a thank you present. He says you inspired him to take his art to a whole new level.

I can't thank you enough for taking the time out this summer to help me. You have transformed my grandsons' lives and bonded my family with glue so strong we'll never drift apart again.

When I count my blessings in future, I'll count you twice.

Until we meet again,

Wilhelmina x

Millie wiped away a tear. How kind of Wilhelmina. She walked back into the main office to see the team back at their desks. Millie felt guilty to ask, but she needed a lift home. Susie and Melanie were her best hope. 'Is there any chance one of you could give me a lift at lunchtime? I need to get home with my new equipment. I told Cynthia I should be online from this afternoon, network permitting.'

Melanie glanced at the painting. 'Do we need to get that back to yours too?'

Millie nodded. 'If you don't mind. Jordan was supposed to help me, but I can't see it fitting into his car. It's not that roomy inside.'

Melanie huffed. 'I can't do it. It'll take half an hour to get to yours. That means another half an hour back, and I must get to the Post Office at lunchtime.'

Susie grabbed her bag. 'Come on; I'll take you now if you're ready.'

The girls took three trips to load Susie's car. Thankfully, she had seats that folded down in the back like Cynthia. Millie climbed into the passenger seat before confessing to Susie, 'I don't need to go to my apartment. I'm staying at Jordan's new place. It's only fifteen minutes away.'

Susie turned to stare at her friend. 'Lucky you!'

Millie looked out of the window as Susie drove out of the car park. 'It's just out of convenience. The electricity's gone off in my apartment, the freezer's defrosted, and the kitchen's flooded.'

Susie grinned. 'Is that so?'

Millie turned to look at Susie. 'Yes!'

Susie smiled to herself. She'd known Millie would

settle down with Jordan. Madame Wilhelmina predicted it at Easter. Apart from saying there were going to be big changes at the place where Susie worked, Madame Wilhelmina had advised that Susie's best friend would marry someone who was "fair". When it looked like Millie had the attention of both Brett and Jordan back in April, Susie's money had always been on tousled blonde Jordan. Millie had hit the jackpot!

*

Jordan arrived back at the office after taking *Ennis Everglades* to lunch. They'd agreed to sign a new contract now that Jordan had taken over from Brett. It was his first day in his new role, and business was picking up already.

29

SURPRISE INVITATION

Six weeks later, Millie and Jordan were settling into a routine. Millie was using a ground-floor room overlooking the front gardens as her office. Jordan had ensured it was one of the first rooms decorated to Millie's taste. *Millie's Summer Collection* hung on the first-floor landing, and the Chad Harbottle portrait took pride of place in the living room.

The *Harbottle Recruitment Agency* was going from strength to strength; Jordan followed employment law to the letter. Four new recruitment consultants were now in place, and an administrator: all with contracts protecting the employees *and* the business.

It was a sunny Friday afternoon when Millie walked down the drive to the post box outside the electric gates. She'd built the post-lunch exercise into her daily routine and enjoyed getting some fresh air in the middle of the day. Millie opened the gates and unlocked the post box to retrieve the mail. There were seven envelopes in today's post; two concerning her job at *Mosely Timmins*; three addressed to Jordan; and two gold envelopes that stood out from the rest – one for her and the other for Jordan. Millie was intrigued to find out what they contained.

When she was back in her office, Millie opened her envelope. A smile lit up her face when she read the gold embossed invitation:

You are cordially invited to attend the Opening Night of the

Harbottle Harbourside Hotel

The English Riviera's Premier Boutique Establishment

on Saturday 14th November at 7.00 p.m.

Dress Code: Black Tie

RSVP: Brett Harbottle (details overleaf)

Millie clapped her hands. Brett had done it! Not only was the hotel re-branded in a record amount of time, but he'd also thought of inviting her and Jordan to the Opening Night. Millie reread the invitation; she'd need to buy a new dress.

Millie was in the kitchen when Jordan arrived home. 'Something smells good. What's for dinner tonight?'

'Spaghetti carbonara.'

'Fantastic.'

Jordan slid his arm around Millie's waist, and she turned to kiss him before waving his gold envelope in the air. 'You need to open this. I've got one too. Go and have a read, then we can talk about it over dinner. It'll be ready in fifteen minutes.'

Jordan rushed upstairs to change, then came back down and lit the fire in the dining room. It was getting colder in the evenings. He drew the curtains, then lit the candles on the table before sniffing the freshly picked flowers Millie had arranged in a short vase. He then sat down and opened the envelope. He smiled when he read the invitation, then unfolded the hand-written note:

> *Dear Jordan*
>
> *We now have a honeymoon suite at the hotel and, of course, we'll offer you mates rates on any wedding package you choose.*
>
> *Brett will show you around when we see you on Opening Night.*
>
> *Yours sincerely*
>
> *Wilhelmina Harbottle*

Jordan shoved the note in his trouser pocket. That

woman was unbelievable! Millie walked into the room with two bowls of carbonara. Jordan poured the wine she'd chosen from the cellar. He was flustered and tried to cover his annoyance by reading the label on the wine bottle. 'Good choice, Millie. A perfect wine to go with spaghetti.'

Millie smiled. 'Have you opened the envelope yet?' Jordan nodded while he chewed. 'Well, I presume you have a dinner jacket. I'll need to buy a new dress.'

Jordan swallowed and then gave her the bad news, 'I'm not going.'

Millie's mouth fell open. 'Why on earth not?'

'Because it'll take up a whole weekend, and I have better things to do.'

Millie was furious. She pushed her bowl to one side and folded her arms. 'I'm very disappointed in you. We owe it to Brett to support him.'

Jordan shook his head as he continued to eat before swallowing again. 'I'm NOT going.'

Millie pushed her chair back and stormed out of the dining room before slamming the door shut. She rushed to their bedroom and gathered her things; she'd move into another room tonight. The only trouble was – only one bedroom had been furnished. Jordan had slept downstairs on a sofa when she'd first moved in.

Millie couldn't very well throw him out of his bedroom; *she'd* have to sleep on the sofa tonight. At this point, Millie was so annoyed she decided to spend the evening in her office until he'd gone to bed.

Jordan was disappointed with Millie's reaction to his decision. She thought more of Brett than of him. What had he done by taking her in? He couldn't care less if he never saw her again, but now she was a permanent fixture. It didn't help that she worked for *Mosely Timmins*; she was also now one of his clients. Brett had made mistakes, but Jordan's were greater by far!

There was nothing else for it; Jordan was going to the pub. The King's Head was within walking distance, and he needed time out. Millie heard the front door slam, and she peeked through her office shutters to see Jordan striding down the driveway. That was a result – it was good to see the back of him.

*

Jordan sat up at the bar and downed a pint of beer. He didn't recognise anyone in the pub tonight. He felt like a loser, so, to be less conspicuous, he ordered another beer and sat down at a table. That move didn't help at all – his heart cracked. He was sitting at the table he'd been sitting at with Millie when he'd offered to move in with her six months ago. He thought back to Millie all alone in his home. She'd be hungry by now; she hadn't eaten dinner. Why had things gone so wrong tonight? If Jordan were honest with himself, he'd have jumped at the chance of taking Millie to the Opening Night of the *Harbottle Harbourside Hotel* – it was just the note from Wilhelmina that had scared him off.

Jordan took another sip of beer. What would it be like being married to Millie? His heart sank when he realised he'd never been happier in his life than just before their silly argument. There were paintings of Millie all over the place in his home, and he liked that. He loved looking into her cornflower blue eyes with the sea and sunset behind her; Chad had captured her perfectly. When Jordan thought about it – really thought about it – he wanted nothing more than to be married to Millie. He needed to get home; couples should never go to sleep on an argument.

*

With Jordan out of the way, Millie cleared up the kitchen. She couldn't concentrate on doing anything else. At least she'd hear when Jordan came home so she could dart back into her office.

Millie entered the dining room to retrieve the bowls and glasses from earlier. She put a guard around the dwindling fire and bent down to blow out the candles. As Millie did so, she noticed a folded-up piece of paper at the foot of Jordan's chair. She picked it up and held it next to a candle to read it. Her heart sank;

Wilhelmina had frightened Jordan off. What on earth was the woman playing at?

The front door opened, and Jordan took his coat off before going in search of Millie. He found her in the dining room with the note in her hand. She smiled at him. 'Now I know why you don't want to return to the hotel. Why didn't you tell me about this?'

Jordan was relieved Millie had calmed down. It made it easier to apologise. 'I'm sorry, Millie, I got cold feet. It was more of a shock than anything. I hadn't thought about marriage yet. I guess I just needed a nudge.'

Millie frowned. 'What do you mean?'

Jordan got down on one knee. 'Will you marry me, Millie? I can't imagine life without you. There are paintings of you all over this house, and I wouldn't want it any other way. Besides, we'll get mates rates at the *Harbottle Harbourside Hotel* and use of the new honeymoon suite if you say "yes".'

Millie's heart leapt. 'Will I get a ring?'

Jordan stood up and held her in his arms. 'Wilhelmina shocked me to my senses tonight – I didn't have time to prepare. If you say "yes", then we'll go to Hatton Garden tomorrow, and you can choose whatever ring you like.'

'Is there a budget?'

'No budget.'

'In that case, it's a definite YES!'

Jordan bent his head to kiss Millie, and she held a finger to his lips. 'There's just one condition to all of this – we go to the Opening Night of the *Harbottle Harbourside Hotel*.'

Jordan smiled. 'Of course, that's not in question. I thought you were going to say you wanted Brett to play the piano at our wedding.'

Millie giggled. 'Now there's a thought.'

30

OPENING NIGHT

The drive to Devon in the middle of November wasn't as pleasurable as the journey in June. Rain lashed against the windscreen of Jordan's Porsche, and there was one traffic jam after another.

Millie checked the time. 'I can't believe we set off at ten this morning. We should have been there by mid-afternoon, it's nearly six o'clock, and we've still got ten miles to go.'

Jordan reached over and patted Millie's knee. 'It just means we'll have less time to get ready. I'll have a quick shower as soon as we get there, then I can meet up with Brett downstairs to hatch our plan.'

Millie admired her vintage engagement ring. She knew she could have any ring she wanted from Hatton Garden, but that wasn't her style. Millie had seen the perfect ring in a local jewellery store months ago; she was just relieved it had still been there the day after Jordan proposed.

It was six-thirty when Jordan wheeled an overnight bag into their hotel room. There was a bottle of champagne on the coffee table and a note from Brett:

Welcome back, you two!
Glad you could make it.
See you in the bar just before seven. Brett

Jordan popped the champagne. 'Good old Brett.'

Millie got changed and touched up her make-up. Jordan had insisted on buying her a red satin ballgown; it was strapless with a full skirt and narrow diamante waistband. Jordan dashed out of the shower, towel dried his hair and threw on his clothes. He stood in front of Millie, holding his arms out for her to insert his cufflinks. Millie looked up at her fiancé. He was more handsome than ever tonight. His blonde hair was still damp but would return to its tousled look when it dried out.

Jordan finished his glass of champagne before kissing Millie on the top of her head – he didn't want to smudge her red lipstick. 'I must go. Try not to leave me down there too long on my own. I won't be able to keep our secret.' Jordan flew out of the room and then opened the door again. 'You look amazing, by the way.'

He blew a kiss before dashing off.

Millie piled her hair high and fixed it with diamante clips. She'd been practising the style all week. It didn't look too bad when she loosened a few tendrils to fall around her face and down her neck. Millie fastened her strappy silver stilettos and grabbed her matching bag before rushing out of the room. She was halfway down the corridor when she bumped into Wilhelmina.

'Millie! It's good to see you.' Wilhelmina kissed Mille on both cheeks before frowning. 'I don't like your hair like that, dear. It looks so much better down. It's a special night for you; you must look your best.'

Millie's knuckles went white as she gripped her bag with both hands. That was better than gripping the annoying woman's neck. What was wrong with her hair? Suddenly one of the loose tendrils turned into an avalanche, and Millie struggled to see.

Wilhelmina smiled. 'There, I was right. I'll come back to your room with you, and we can brush it out.'

Millie sat at her dressing table while Wilhelmina brushed her hair. She couldn't believe she was letting her do this; the interfering woman had nearly broken her and Jordan up. Wilhelmina was humming as she brushed, and Millie felt bad about being so hard on her. The humming stopped, and Millie looked in the mirror; Wilhelmina's face had drained of colour. The humming started up again and ended when the brushing stopped.

'There, you look so much better now, dear. We should go downstairs and get the party started.'

*

Jordan was propping up the bar with Brett. 'So, you see, Brett, I don't care if you have any special offers available or not. Millie and I won't be forced into marriage by you or your grandmother. You'll have to look elsewhere to bring in some business. How's it going, by the way?'

When Millie neared the bottom of the stairs, she switched her engagement ring from her left hand to her right. The Harbottle family thought they could interfere in people's lives; they needed to be put in their place.

Danny and Chad stood at the foot of the stairs, and Brett shooed them away. 'It's not going to plan – Granny will be livid.'

Millie glided over to stand next to Jordan. He wanted to take her in his arms and announce to the whole world they were engaged, but he'd have to wait until they'd made a stand against the manipulating busybodies. Millie looked stunning tonight; he was glad she'd decided to leave her hair down.

Brett gestured to his grandmother and brothers to

join him in his office. He shut the door and grimaced. Danny raised his eyebrows. 'What's the matter?'

Brett sighed. 'We've overdone it with trying to push them together. Jordan's having none of it. If anything, I think we're pushing them apart. Jordan would have proposed by now of his own accord if that's what he wanted to do.'

Chad was disappointed in their grandmother. He chose not to bring up the fact he'd warned her against messing with affairs of the heart. 'What are we going to do now? You'd predicted tonight would turn into an engagement party. There's a cake and everything.'

Wilhelmina lowered her eyes. 'Things have taken their natural course; we didn't need to interfere. They're tricking us – they're already engaged.'

Brett punched the air, and Chad and Danny high-fived. They returned to the bar while Wilhelmina sat down and composed her thoughts.

Millie was wearing a ring that Wilhelmina had lost last Easter. She'd put it in her diamante bag for good luck when she participated in the salsa competition with Wilfred. It was her mother's engagement ring. Wilhelmina remembered her mother wearing it when she'd taken her to dance competitions when she was a little girl; the ring was special to her.

Still, time moves on. Wilhelmina didn't have any

granddaughters to leave it to, and it was fitting the lost ring had found its way to Millie. Wilhelmina couldn't bear to be totally without it, though, and she went to find Chad. 'Make sure you take photographs when they cut the cake and get a close-up of the ring. You can do me a small painting of it for Christmas. I used to have a similar ring, and it would give me great pleasure to keep a memento of it on my dressing table.'

Chad didn't ask any questions. What his grandmother wanted, she got.

31

CONFESSION TIME

Brett was now seated at the piano, playing a medley of Michael Bublé songs. Millie swooned. 'I love Michael Bublé. You're lucky he's not available.' Millie turned to whisper in Jordan's ear, 'Otherwise, I may not have agreed to marry you.'

Jordan grinned and brushed his lips against the side of her hair as he pretended to reach for something on the bar. Danny nudged Chad. 'They won't be able to keep this up for long. They're so starry-eyed they haven't even noticed that Millie's the only one wearing a ballgown – and we're the only fools in bow-ties.'

Half an hour later, Millie was hungry. 'Do you think there'll be any food at this party? Shouldn't Brett be mingling with the guests and showing people around? He's not going to bring in business by just sitting there playing the piano.'

Jordan glanced around the room. 'We've been stitched up.'

Millie frowned. 'What do you mean?'

'You're the only one in a ballgown, and I'm the only one in a dinner jacket — well, apart from the Harbottle brothers. All of them are pretending not to look at us. They're just waiting to pounce as soon as we come clean with our good news.'

Millie looked around the room and then at Wilhelmina, who was wearing a black knee-length knitted dress with a row of pearls. Millie was horrified. 'What are we going to do? I stand out like a sore thumb.'

Jordan cringed. 'It looks like we're at a stalemate. Our plan has backfired, and theirs has gone up in smoke.'

Wilhelmina made the first move. She walked over to kiss Millie and shake Jordan's hand. 'I am so pleased you two are engaged. You should have invited us to the party.'

Millie smiled. 'Thank you. How did you work it out? It only happened recently, and we didn't have a party.'

'You were wearing a pretty ring on your engagement finger earlier. I saw it when I was brushing your hair.'

Millie glanced down at her hands and swapped the ring back. 'We were trying to keep it a surprise. We were going to tell you later.'

The piano music stopped, and the Harbottle brothers walked over to congratulate the happy couple. Brett had a confession to make, 'You've probably worked out you're the only ones invited here tonight. The hotel isn't fully refurbished yet. It won't be ready until February. So far, we've only changed the name and knocked a couple of rooms together to make a honeymoon suite.'

Millie was confused. 'So why invite us here tonight?'

Wilhelmina held her shoulders back. 'Because I couldn't wait much longer for Jordan to propose. I knew he'd get down on one knee when he saw you in a ballgown. Wilfred didn't do a very good job of *our* engagement; he's always had dodgy knees.' Wilhelmina lowered her eyes before continuing, 'We didn't have an acceptable wedding either; it was a low-key affair. I was hoping Millie's experience would be better than mine.'

Jordan was shocked Wilhelmina was being so open; his opinion of her was beginning to soften. 'Well, you'll be pleased to hear I *did* get down on one knee when I proposed. To be honest with you, Wilhelmina,

I'm struggling to understand why you're so keen to rush things along?'

Wilhelmina sighed. 'Because we need to get your wedding booked in. We're running out of dates.'

Millie grabbed Jordan's hands and smiled up at him. 'What do you think?'

'I think we should go and see what the honeymoon suite's like before we make a decision.'

Wilhelmina did a little clap. 'Excellent. I'll lead the way. Come along, everyone.'

*

The honeymoon suite didn't disappoint; it had a four-poster bed, champagne-coloured silk sheets, a bathroom with a double shower, twin sinks, and a whirlpool bath. It led out onto a roof terrace with spectacular sea views. It was dark now, but the promenade was lit up, and the sea was visible from the light of a full moon and canopy of twinkling stars. Jordan looked over the balcony. 'We're higher up than the penthouse suite.'

Wilhelmina twirled her pearl necklace around her fingers. Millie hoped it wouldn't break, sending the pearls flying everywhere. Wilhelmina guessed what the young woman was thinking. 'Don't worry. These are South Sea pearls, and they're worth a fortune. Strings of pearls like these never break; besides each pearl is knotted in place.'

Brett, Chad, and Danny couldn't wipe the grins from their faces. They sensed their grandmother was about to share her news with Millie and Jordan. Wilhelmina continued, 'The area we're standing in now used to be my parents' accommodation. You could say I provided them with a "Granny Annex" in their later life. I must admit I hadn't been into this part of the building since my parents passed away until I met you both last Easter.'

Millie's eyes widened. 'Where do *we* come into it?'

'I knew straight away you'd be married within a year. Of course, I hoped you'd hold your wedding here at the hotel, and I set about renovating this area as a honeymoon suite. As it turns out, my parents had a treasure trove of rare artefacts and jewellery of which I was unaware. They had locked everything away in a spare room.'

Danny continued the story, 'So that's how we were able to buy out Miller and Casey and commence the refurbishment of the hotel.'

Wilhelmina gestured to Millie and Jordan. 'Come with us now. We want to throw a small party to celebrate your engagement. I have a private room booked downstairs.'

Jordan slid Millie's ring off her finger before smiling at Wilhelmina. 'I didn't propose as well as I could have done. I hadn't bought a ring in advance. I want to get it right now.'

Jordan knelt on one knee. 'Will you marry me, Millie? I can't imagine life without you. I suggest we get married at the *Harbottle Harbourside Hotel*; it's the English Riviera's Premier Boutique Establishment. What do you say?'

Millie smiled at her handsome fiancé in his bow-tie and dinner jacket before responding, 'YES!'

Brett was impressed that Jordan had remembered the wording he'd used on tonight's invite. Wilhelmina discretely removed her handkerchief from her sleeve when she saw Jordan pushing her mother's ring onto Millie's finger. Now that she knew her parents hadn't been short of money and had invested in priceless artefacts, including jewellery, she predicted that Millie's engagement ring was worth a fortune.

Jordan whispered in Wilhelmina's ear as they left the terrace, 'I've heard of holding someone over a barrel. Please tell me you weren't going to hold me over that balcony until I proposed to Millie.'

Wilhelmina's eyes twinkled. 'No, dear. You wouldn't have taken that much persuading.'

32

A WEDDING TO PLAN

The following morning, Jordan retrieved a note from under the door. He opened the envelope and read the message:

Dear Millie and Jordan,

I'll be in the beach house all day. Please come to see me before you leave.

Regards, Chad

Jordan handed the note to Millie, who raised her eyebrows. 'I wonder what Chad wants? We said "goodbye" to everyone last night.'

There was a knock on the door, and Jordan opened it. Their room service breakfast had arrived. Jordan signalled for it to be laid out on a table by the window overlooking the sea. When the hotel staff had left,

Jordan took hold of Millie's hand across the table. 'None of this pressurised wedding planning sits well with me.'

Millie knew Jordan was unhappy. She squeezed his hand before responding, 'Me neither. I can't believe the only date they have available next year is the 14th of February. I thought Valentine's Day would be the first to go. I know venues get booked up well in advance, but something doesn't feel right about this.'

Jordan kept hold of Millie's hand; he needed to challenge things and didn't want a row like the last time he'd refused to do something. 'If you had your choice of any type of wedding, what would you choose?'

Millie sighed before responding, 'I've always wanted a white wedding with lots of snow. I wouldn't want a huge affair. I'd be happy if it were just the two of us – I don't like a fuss.'

Jordan stood up and pulled Millie into his arms. 'That sounds perfect to me. The only problem would be the guaranteed snow, but I have an idea.' Jordan let go of Millie and picked up his phone. She could see him searching for something on the internet. Breakfast was going cold, so Millie sat down and tucked into her bacon and eggs. Jordan was taking charge of things, and it felt such a relief.

Millie had finished her breakfast when Jordan put

his phone down and started eating his. She stared at him. 'You can't eat that – it's cold.'

Jordan sliced through his fried egg. 'It may be cold, but it's the best breakfast I've ever tasted.'

Millie stared into her fiancé's sparkling grey eyes, and her stomach leapt with excitement. Jordan was devising a plan. After drinking his cold coffee, he stood up. 'We'd best get a move on if we're going to the beach house before we leave. I've got a lot to sort out when we get home.'

*

Chad was relieved to see Millie and Jordan. Sensitive issues were best dealt with in person. He took them up to his mezzanine floor and offered them freshly brewed coffee. 'Let's sit around the kitchen table.'

Millie and Jordan did as Chad suggested and were surprised to see a framed black and white photograph propped up in the centre of the table. Millie strained her eyes. 'Is that a picture of your grandparents?' Jordan picked up the frame and scrutinised the photograph. He held it closer to read a handwritten note at the bottom:

My Wedding to Wilfred on Valentine's Day

Chad arrived with the coffees. He took a deep breath before speaking, 'Out of all us boys, I'm the most observant. When my grandmother advised you last night that Valentine's Day was the only day next year the hotel could host your wedding, I knew she was being less than truthful.'

Millie grabbed Jordan's hand and he put the frame down on the table while he listened to Chad's revelations. 'My grandparents were married on Valentine's Day sixty years ago next year. I'm concerned my grandmother is trying to use you both to satisfy a gap in her life. I've advised her in the past about messing with affairs of the heart.'

Jordan's grey eyes twinkled. 'We're very appreciative of receiving this inside information, Chad. It helps greatly.'

Millie's eyes were on stalks. 'Last night, Wilhelmina made it clear she wasn't happy with her engagement; or her wedding.'

Chad nodded. 'Exactly.'

Jordan rubbed his hands together. 'I have an idea.'

Millie turned to face him. 'What's that?'

'We keep Valentine's Day clear in the diary at the hotel and don't tell Wilhelmina what the event's really for.' Millie raised her eyebrows, and Jordan winked at Chad. 'I need to make some calls this afternoon to ensure Millie has the wedding of her dreams, but I also want Wilhelmina to have the wedding celebration she never had.'

Millie couldn't help but ask, 'What will happen on Valentine's Day at the hotel?'

Jordan grinned. 'A Diamond Wedding celebration; the best seen on the English Riviera.' Jordan stood up and shook Chad's hand. 'I'll leave you to sort out the logistics with your brothers. I have a private wedding to plan. Just make sure we get invites on Valentine's Day.'

Chad's eyes were alight. 'You certainly will.'

33

ONE DAY TO GO

Three months later, Millie rested her head on Jordan's shoulder. The last five days had been the best of her life. Eloping to Lapland had been a wonderful experience, and the newly married couple were now on a plane home to London.

Jordan stroked his wife's face. 'Tell me your favourite parts.'

'The ceremony in the ice chapel, hunting the Northern Lights in that horse-drawn sleigh, the champagne dinner in front of a fire in a glass tepee. And the snow – there was so much snow! What about you?'

'The dog sledding was cool, snowshoeing to the chapel was hilarious, and having hardly any daylight, was out of this world.'

'Is that it?'

'I must admit I enjoyed feeding the reindeer; I never knew how much moss they could eat.'

The couple were interrupted by an announcement from the pilot: 'Due to adverse weather conditions, we are unable to land in London. We are trying to get a slot in Edinburgh. I will update you as soon as we have more news.'

Millie dug her nails into Jordan's arm. 'But we *have* to get to Devon by tomorrow!'

*

At the *Harbottle Harbourside Hotel*, things were going to plan. Wilhelmina was supervising the preparations for "Millie and Jordan's wedding". She felt honoured that Millie had given her free rein to choose the menu, the flowers and devise the seating plan. Wilhelmina was surprised that no family members were coming for Millie and Jordan. It was a shame they had to make up the numbers with staff from the recruitment agency and hotel, still, it wasn't her place to be nosy. She was just grateful they were using the hotel for their special day.

It was mid-morning when Chad presented his grandmother with a large white box. Wilhelmina glanced at him. 'What do you have there?'

'A present from Millie.'

Wilhelmina stared at the box before opening the lid. There was a card inside:

Dear Wilhelmina

You need to wear this dress tomorrow it will look great in the photos.

Love Millie xxx

Wilhelmina unfolded the tissue paper and then stared at Chad. 'I can't wear this. It's white.'

Chad shrugged his shoulders. 'Millie should get what *she* wants tomorrow. You need to wear the dress.'

*

Susie was on a train with Melanie. 'This is so exciting. I can't believe we've been invited to a "Celebration" at the *Harbottle Harbourside Hotel*. It was lucky you noticed Jordan had written "Wedding Day" in his diary before he deleted it. How romantic to get married on Valentine's Day!'

*

The pilot made another announcement: 'I am pleased to advise we will be landing in Edinburgh in fifteen minutes. I apologise for any inconvenience caused by matters beyond our control.'

Jordan squeezed Millie's hand. 'Don't worry. We'll get the overnight train from Edinburgh to London, then drive to Devon in the morning.'

Millie's head was pounding. This wasn't how it was supposed to turn out – they'd be shattered by the time they got to the hotel. Why couldn't things be simple?

*

In the taxi on the way from the airport to the station, Jordan called Brett. 'Yes, thanks, we had a great time … Have you managed to keep our secret from Wilhelmina? … Good … The only trouble is our flight home has landed in Edinburgh … I know! … What are the chances of that? … We're on our way to the station to get the overnight train to London … We'll see you tomorrow, but we'll be arriving later than planned.'

At the station, the train destined for London was pulling away from the platform. Millie wanted to cry. Jordan put his arm around her. 'That's not a problem. I'll work out another way to get us there. Let's go and grab a coffee, and I'll assess our options.'

*

Susie and Melanie dragged their overnight bags through the hotel's foyer. Wilhelmina walked over to greet them. 'Are you here for tomorrow's wedding?'

Melanie grinned at Susie. There it was!

Confirmation that Millie and Jordan would be walking down the aisle tomorrow. Before they could answer, Brett joined Wilhelmina. 'Hi, girls. It's great you could make it down here for tomorrow's celebration. Let me take my grandmother to her room. She needs her beauty sleep.'

Brett linked arms with Wilhelmina and escorted her to the lift. 'You've been working too hard on tomorrow's party. There are bags under your eyes. Get an early night, and don't surface until I come and get you in the morning.'

With his grandmother in the lift, Brett breathed a sigh of relief. The brothers had managed to keep the secret of their grandparents' special day up until now. They couldn't risk anything going wrong at the eleventh hour.

Brett joined Susie and Melanie. 'Let me buy you both a drink. What was the weather like in London? Millie and Jordan are stranded in Edinburgh. Their flight back from Lapland was diverted.'

Melanie gasped. 'Lapland?! It says in Jordan's diary he's at a conference in Cardiff.'

Brett held his head in his hands. He'd been doing so well – up until now. 'Forget I said that.'

Melanie raised an eyebrow. 'Why?'

'Because I'm under a lot of pressure with keeping secrets. All will become clear by tomorrow afternoon. Keep your heads down, and don't get me into trouble.'

Susie giggled. 'It sounds like the old days when you were our boss.'

Melanie grinned. 'A bottle of champagne should keep us quiet.'

Brett held out his hand to shake Melanie's. 'It's a deal.'

*

How difficult could it be to get to the English Riviera? Millie and Jordan were now on a flight to Dublin . . .

34

SURPRISE CEREMONY

The following morning Brett received another call from Jordan. 'Hi, mate. Where are you both now? What a shame the weather around London was bad yesterday. It's been sunny here all week.'

Jordan kept his voice low; Millie was in the shower, and he didn't want her to hear, 'We're in Dublin. We stayed at an airport hotel last night. I managed to get us a flight to Plymouth this morning, but we're going to be pushing it to get there in time for the ceremony. It's been a bit of a nightmare; Millie bought a great dress to wear, but we can't get home to pick it up.'

Brett rubbed his chin. 'We could always delay things.'

Jordan scratched his head. 'No. Don't do that. It's

Wilhelmina's day today.'

Brett felt anxious. 'What will Granny say when she doesn't see the "bride" this morning? She'll want to help Millie with her hair and make-up – or whatever women do on the mornings of weddings.'

'You'll need to tell a white lie. Say that Millie wants to make a grand entrance in a wedding car, so she's getting ready at a hotel around the corner.'

'That's a great idea. Try not to be too late. See you soon!'

Millie walked out of the bathroom with a towel wrapped around her head. 'Who were you on the phone to?'

Jordan lowered his eyes. 'Oh, just the help desk at Dublin Airport. I was checking whether they have dresses in your size in any of the shops.'

Millie frowned. 'And have they?'

'Have they what?'

'Got dresses in my size in the airport shops.'

'Of course. We should aim to get there early so you can try some on.'

*

Wilhelmina paced around her bedroom; she didn't like

it when she wasn't in control. It was a great disappointment Millie had chosen to get ready at a hotel around the corner. It also didn't help that Brett made her feel like a spare part by insisting she had to stay in her room until he came to get her. At least Wilfred was enjoying himself. He'd got ready early and given her a big cuddle before he'd left the room. She couldn't remember when Wilfred had last given her a cuddle like that. She wasn't surprised he'd forgotten it was their anniversary – Wilfred never bought a card.

All the guests were seated in the ceremony room by two-thirty; Brett walked down the aisle before turning to face everyone. 'I would like to thank you all for coming here today for this celebration. Some of you have ideas about what's going to happen, but none of you will have guessed the real reason we are gathered here today.'

Melanie whispered to Susie, 'He sounds like a vicar.'

Brett continued, 'We are all members of the Harbottle family, and today is an exceptional day – it's my grandparents' Diamond Wedding Anniversary.' Brett paused while the chatter and gasps around the room subsided. 'Wilhelmina and Wilfred Harbottle were married sixty years ago on Valentine's Day, and we thought it would be a nice idea to have a surprise celebration. The person who will be most surprised is my grandmother; she thinks she's been organising a wedding. With that said, I'd like to introduce you to my grandfather, who's in on the secret.'

That was the sign for Wilfred to walk down the aisle to whistles and cheers. He was grinning from ear to ear as he undertook a few salsa moves while he waved at the smiling crowd; his new hip was performing well.

Brett remained with his grandfather while Chad and Danny went to collect their grandmother. Wilhelmina was surprised to see them. 'What are you two doing here? I'm waiting for Brett.'

Wilhelmina looked very glamorous in her long white lace dress. Danny winked at her. 'You look gorgeous. Even better than on your wedding day – well, from the photos I've seen.'

Chad kissed his grandmother on her cheek. 'I agree with Danny. Come along. We're here to walk you down the aisle.'

'But I'm walking down before Millie. It's all arranged. We can't all walk down together. Is Millie here yet?' Chad and Danny linked arms with their reluctant grandmother and dragged her out of her room.

Wilhelmina was in shock. She stepped out of the lift to see Millie and Jordan running into the building. Millie ran straight up to her. She was wearing a long blue lace dress, and her wavy hair fell loose around her shoulders. Wilhelmina threw her arms around the young woman. 'I don't know what's going on. My grandsons have seriously messed things up. Why aren't you wearing a wedding dress?'

The Head Receptionist appeared with two posies of flowers. Wilhelmina looked at Millie. 'I ordered these for us, as you asked me to be your Matron of Honour.'

Millie took hold of the posies and handed the larger one to Wilhelmina. 'Well, we're changing roles. I'm going to be *your* Matron of Honour.'

Wilhelmina shook her head. 'No, dear, you can't be that you're not married.'

Jordan stepped forward. 'We were married in Lapland three days ago. Millie wanted a white wedding, with snow, reindeer, diverted flights, nightmare journey home, that type of thing.'

Wilhelmina's mouth fell open, and Millie bent down to straighten the small train on the older woman's dress. 'Don't listen to him. We had a wonderful time, and I'll tell you about it later. We should get a move on now. It's not good to keep Wilfred waiting.'

*

Brett played a classical piece on the piano as his brothers walked Wilhelmina down the aisle. When she reached the end, she linked arms with her husband. For once, she was lost for words. 'I don't know what to say. I have nothing prepared.'

Brett stood to face the guests, and Chad and Danny took their places beside him. 'Neither of you needs to say anything. We've prepared the speeches. No one knows the pair of you better than us. We have a few memories to share of the best grandparents in the world.'

Melanie whispered to Susie, 'Wilhelmina's an unusual name. You don't think she could be Madame Wilhelmina, do you?'

Susie shook her head before whispering, 'Definitely not. Brett's grandmother wouldn't be a fortune teller.'

'But Madame Wilhelmina told you there would be big changes at the place where you worked.'

'That's correct. But she had no idea *where* I worked. Trust me, Madame Wilhelmina's the real deal – she's not Brett's grandmother.'

Melanie looked dubious, so Susie shared Madame Wilhelmina's other prediction, 'She also told me my best friend would get married to someone who's "fair".'

That caught Melanie's attention. She glanced around the room. 'Really? What do you think of him, two rows in front to the right?'

Susie frowned. 'What are you talking about?'

'Well, if I'm going to marry a blonde, he may be in this room. There's no better place to meet your future husband than at a wedding celebration. There's romance in the air – can't you feel it?'

35

TIME FOR A PARTY

It had taken months of planning to make today a success. Brett clinked glasses with his brothers. 'We did it! We pulled it off.'

Wilhelmina took Millie to one side. 'You did this for me, didn't you, dear?'

Millie smiled. 'I had very little input, apart from being a decoy. Your grandsons worked out it was your Diamond Wedding Anniversary today, and they wanted to do something special.'

'But I gave *you* this date for *your* wedding.'

'I know, but it wouldn't have worked. Ever since I was a little girl, I wanted to get married in the snow. The English Riviera rarely gets snow. Besides, Valentine's Day is special to you and Wilfred.'

Wilhelmina took hold of Millie's left hand. 'Oh, I

do so love your wedding ring. How did you get one to match your vintage engagement ring? It must have been a struggle to find something.'

Millie shook her head. 'It couldn't have been easier. The manager of the local jewellery shop phoned Jordan. He said that something very unusual had happened. A ring had arrived in the post for their pre-loved jewellery section, which matched perfectly with my engagement ring. Of course, we had to buy it.'

Wilhelmina frowned. 'They charged you for it?'

'Of course, they're not going to give rings away for nothing. They have a business to run.'

Wilhelmina scowled, then strained her neck to look over Millie's shoulder. 'What's that girl doing over there with all those blonde men?'

Millie turned to see who the girl was. 'That's Melanie from the agency.'

Wilhelmina looked thoughtful. 'Well, she's wasting her time. I see her marrying a much older man – one with grey hair. Anyway, I want to hear all about your wedding. The honeymoon suite is reserved for you tonight.' Wilhelmina smiled. 'You *will* make sure you bring the babies back here for their summer holidays, won't you, dear?'

Millie blushed. The woman was incorrigible.

Susie threw a hand to her mouth. She'd gone to look for Millie because Melanie had left her stranded; she hadn't meant to eavesdrop on Millie's conversation with Wilhelmina. When Susie had been to see Madame Wilhelmina at Easter, she'd predicted something else that Susie had thought was too far-fetched to believe. Madame Wilhelmina had said that apart from marrying a "fair" man, she could see Susie's best friend "pushing a pram with a blue blanket".

With the party in full swing, Jordan searched the room for Millie. She was easy enough to spot in her long blue lace dress, but he couldn't find her. He went over to ask Brett if he'd seen her, but he was talking to Wilhelmina. Jordan stood a short distance away, waiting for them to finish their conversation.

Brett nodded towards Daisy and Poppy, standing up at the bar. 'So, go on, Granny. What's your prediction about those two? Will Danny or I be the next to get married?'

'You'll get married first. But it won't be to either of those. Danny hasn't found his bride yet either. There's plenty of time for you both. No need to rush.'

Jordan chuckled to himself before his phone vibrated with a message from Millie:

> *Come up to the honeymoon suite. Quick!*
> *You need to see this! Millie xxx*

Jordan didn't wait for the lift; he bounded up the stairs. He was out of breath when he reached the top of the building. Millie was standing on the terrace with flakes of snow in her hair. 'Can you believe it? It's snowing!'

Jordan crossed the terrace to take his wife into his arms. 'We could have had a white wedding here after all.'

Millie smiled up at him. 'But we wouldn't have seen the Northern Lights or fed the reindeer.'

Jordan stroked her damp hair. 'That's true.'

Millie held her husband tightly around his waist. She couldn't wait to tell him her news. 'Wilhelmina wants us to bring our babies back here for their summer holidays.'

Large snowflakes were now settling on Jordan's head. 'Babies? Does that mean we'll be having more than one? When are we having a baby?'

Millie raised her hands in the air. 'Who knows? We'll have to wait and see.'

'Unless we ask for more details from Wilhelmina.'

Millie shook her head. 'I don't want to do that. I want an element of surprise.'

*

The following morning, Wilhelmina hugged Millie and Jordan. 'Make sure you keep in touch. I want to hear all your news.'

Chad took hold of their bags. 'I'll put these in my car. We need to get a move on if you want to catch the eleven o'clock train.'

Brett and Danny stood on the snow-covered promenade to wave their friends off. When they stepped back inside the hotel, brushing fresh snow off their shoulders and wiping their shoes, Wilhelmina pounced. She prodded Brett on his shoulder. 'We need to buy some new cots and highchairs. Two of each should do it.' Wilhelmina rubbed her hands together; it was best to deal with things straight away before she forgot.

Danny smirked, and Brett raised his eyebrows; their grandmother was one of a kind.

36

THE FAIR RETURNS

Six weeks later, the fair was back in the field behind Millie's old apartment, and Susie couldn't resist another visit to Madame Wilhelmina. She stood in a queue until it was her turn to go in. When Susie walked into the hut, she saw the black shrouded body. 'Please turn the sign on the door. We must not be disturbed. What do you want to know, my dear?'

The voice was low and slow, and Susie gripped her hands together in her lap. 'I came to see you last year, and most of what you told me has come true.'

'What did I predict, my dear?'

'You said there would be big changes where I work, and that Millie would marry a "fair" person. That all came true. You also said Millie would be pushing a pram with a blue blanket. I'll have to wait a bit longer to see if you got that right. I've come back to see you today to find out if you know what's going to happen to me.'

The shrouded body let out a sigh. 'I remember you now. I predicted your best friend would marry someone who was fair. I didn't mention the name "Millie".'

'But Millie's my best friend.'

The head under the black veil shook from side to side. 'You are very close to your mother, and the meaning of "fair" doesn't always refer to looks. It can depict nature.'

Susie gripped the edge of her chair while she gathered her thoughts. Her mother had re-married last year. Grey-haired Gordon was the fairest man you could wish to meet. Susie had been delighted when her mother said she was marrying him. Susie frowned. Madame Wilhelmina had got the next bit wrong. Her mother was far too old to have a baby boy.

Madame Wilhelmina pre-empted Susie's thoughts, and she stared into her crystal ball before raising her head. 'I also predicted your best friend would be pushing a pram with a blue blanket – I did not mention that it was *her* baby in the pram.'

Susie gasped. She'd been trying for a baby with her husband for the last three years. 'Is the baby going to be mine?'

The shrouded head nodded. 'Yes, dear.'

*

One year later, Millie sat in a coffee shop with Susie. 'We're taking up so much room with my double buggy and your pram. It'll be a relief when the little ones can sit in highchairs. At least we'll be able to line them up with some toys while we enjoy our coffees.

Susie glanced down at her baby. 'I can't believe Charlie's six weeks old already. Time flies.'

Millie smiled. 'I know. Lulu and Louis are nearly four months! They'll be crawling by the time we go to the English Riviera in the summer.'

Susie giggled. 'Good luck with that! Two babies crawling at once. It's lovely you're going back to Devon again. So much has happened since you won your raffle prize. Your life changed in an instant.'

Millie thought back to Easter two years ago. If she hadn't switched on the TV while eating her ready meal, she wouldn't have met Wilhelmina or commenced the journey that led to such an incredible twist of fate.

Susie finished her coffee. 'Well, one thing's for sure, I'm not going to see Madame Wilhelmina again this weekend. I find her quite scary. I've been to see her the last two years, and her predictions have all come true. Will you and Jordan be going to the fair over Easter?'

Millie frowned. She'd been too busy with the twins to even think about the annual fair. She'd also missed it last year; she was laid low with morning sickness for the whole of Easter. Millie was surprised Wilhelmina hadn't mentioned she was in the area; she would have invited her over for coffee. The house looked splendid now the renovation work was complete. Jordan had accomplished his mission of restoring their Victorian home to her former glory. Millie was proud of her family and their "forever home", and she wanted to show it off.

*

That evening when the babies were asleep in their cots, Jordan opened a bottle of wine. He poured two glasses and brought them into the living room before handing one to Millie. She smiled up at him, and Jordan counted his blessings. He looked around the room at the freshly-picked flowers, the flickering fire in the hearth and the subtly-lit painting of Millie with the wind in her hair outside the Beachside Bistro. Jordan thought back to Brett's catastrophe with Greta and chuckled. Never in a million years could Jordan have predicted he would be here now in his dream home, with Millie as his wife.

Millie sipped her wine. 'Aren't you going to sit down? Why are you laughing?'

Jordan sat on the sofa and slid his arm around Millie's shoulders. 'Remember Greta?'

Millie snorted. 'How could I forget?'

Jordan stroked his wife's face as he gazed into her eyes. 'I couldn't be happier than I am right now. It's amazing how things have turned out.'

Millie turned to stare into the fire. 'Susie was saying the same thing earlier. She said my life "changed in an instant" when I won the raffle prize. She's also convinced Madame Wilhelmina's the real thing, not Brett's grandmother. I didn't disappoint her. We all know what Wilhelmina does – she just tells people what they want to hear.'

Millie sat forward and placed her wine glass on the coffee table. 'Anyway, I'm annoyed with Wilhelmina. Why doesn't she tell us when she's in the area? I'd love to show her our home.' Millie picked up her phone. 'I'm going to call her now. It's after nine, and she'll have finished her shift in the hut.'

Wilhelmina answered her phone after two rings, 'Hello, Millie, is there something wrong?'

'No, there's nothing to worry about. We're all fine. I was just calling to complain that you don't let us know when you're in the area. We'd love you to come and see our home. It's Victorian, and we've restored her to her former glory.'

'There's no need to complain, dear. I'm not in your area; I'm in Devon.'

Millie gasped. 'Why aren't you at the Easter fair in the field behind my old apartment?'

Wilhelmina sighed. 'Because my grandsons want me to slow down, and the only way I can do that is by giving up my hobby. Besides, I don't need it anymore. It served a purpose.'

Millie raised her eyebrows at Jordan. 'Oh, I see. Well, I'm sure your clients will be disappointed.'

Wilhelmina changed the subject. 'That's enough about me, dear. How are little Lulu and Louis?'

'They're doing really well, thank you, and growing far too fast. What would you like them to call you when they start talking?'

There was a pause before Wilhelmina spoke, 'What about "Mina"? My mother used to call me that when I was in her good books.'

Millie grinned. 'That's perfect!'

'Oh, and just so you know, the boys want to be uncles.'

'What? Uncle Brett, Uncle Chad, and Uncle Danny?'

'Correct.'

'That's perfect too!' Millie could hear Louis crying on the baby monitor. She didn't want him to wake Lulu. 'I have to go; Louis has woken up. We'll be down to Devon to see you soon. Bye for now.'

37

A FAMILY HOLIDAY

Jordan closed the boot of the family car. These days the Porsche was only used for work. 'Are you sure we've got everything? We seem to be travelling light.'

Millie sat in the front passenger seat. 'We have everything we need. Wilhelmina's set us up in a family suite at the hotel. She's bought cots, highchairs, toys, balance bikes . . . '

'Balance bikes?! The twins aren't crawling yet.'

Millie giggled. 'Well, it just means we'll have to go back again next year – and the year after – Wilhelmina's not stupid.'

Jordan jumped into the car and fastened his seat belt before glancing sideways at Millie. 'Don't tell me Uncle Brett's giving piano lessons on Tuesday afternoon; Uncle Chad's planning an art class on Wednesday morning, and Uncle Danny's lined up for maths and legal sessions on Thursday.'

Millie kept a straight face. 'Uncle Danny will be teaching reading and writing. He's written three books.'

'Three books! I never knew Danny had it in him.'

Jordan turned on the ignition and headed down the gravel drive. 'Our children have very talented uncles. That's summer camp sorted when they're older!'

*

Wilhelmina and the uncles waited in the hotel foyer for the family to arrive; they were due in less than ten minutes if traffic permitted. Danny frowned. 'Do you think they've got any hair yet?'

Chad nodded. 'It should be coming through now. They're six months old.'

Brett took out his wallet. 'Let's take bets. I guess Lulu will have black hair, and Louis will be blonde like Jordan.'

Danny reached for his wallet, and Wilhelmina slapped his arm. 'Stop being so childish. They'll be here shortly.'

Wilhelmina went to the cloakroom, and Brett took the bets. 'OK, twenty pounds each, that's sixty for the winner. To confirm, I bet Lulu has black hair and Louis blonde; Chad thinks black hair for both, and Danny is convinced they'll still be bald.'

Within minutes a large family car pulled up outside the front entrance, and Millie jumped out. She called to Jordan, 'Be quick; there are traffic wardens on patrol. Just get the babies out; we can offload our luggage later.'

The babies arrived in the foyer in their car seats, and Wilhelmina was ecstatic. 'Hello, you two. Aren't you both so gorgeous?'

Millie unclasped Lulu's car seat and handed the little girl to Wilhelmina. Millie then handed Louis to Brett, who held the baby at arm's length. 'What am I supposed to do with him?'

Danny nudged Chad. 'We all lost. They've got brown hair. We need to make sure we get our money back from Brett.'

Wilhelmina's life was complete. She rested her cheek against Lulu's soft hair and wished for her and Louis to have all the happiness in the world. Brett interrupted the magical moment. 'So what am I supposed to do with this baby?!'

*

Two days later, the families were in a routine. Wilhelmina was on constant hand to help out, and so were two of the uncles. Chad had mastered the task of warming milk bottles and feeding the babies and Danny was able to change nappies – well, someone had to do it. Brett was too busy at the hotel to commit to anything.

Millie and Jordan sat on the floor of the family suite with Chad and Danny. Chad had built a tower of bricks, and Lulu and Louis were rocking on their knees trying to reach it. Chad smiled. 'Those two will be off soon.'

Millie sighed. 'Tell me about it; once they're crawling, we'll get no peace.'

Danny had an idea. 'Why don't you two have a romantic dinner for two tonight? Chad and I can babysit. We know how to make bottles and change nappies.'

Jordan glanced at Millie. 'That's a great idea. We won't be long, and we can get the twins bathed and into their cots before we leave. You shouldn't have anything to do apart from eat popcorn and watch sport on TV.'

The brothers stood up. 'What time should we pop back?'

Jordan looked at Millie, who answered on their behalf, 'Well, I suppose it should be OK. We haven't left them with anyone before. We could book a table downstairs for seven-thirty and be back by nine if that suits you?'

Danny grinned. 'See you just before seven-thirty.'

*

Babysitting was a doddle. There was an England rugby match on TV. Chad and Danny sat with their feet up to enjoy it. Two baby monitors on the coffee table gave them views of the babies' cots.

One of the screens on the monitors flashed – a baby was moving. Was it Lulu or Louis? The baby turned around and ended up with its head at the foot of the cot. Danny was worried. 'We should go in and check on them and turn the baby back the right way. They shouldn't move so much in their cots. One of them is being naughty.'

Chad and Danny tiptoed into the adjoining room and weren't surprised that Louis was the "naughty" one. They peered into his cot, and he rolled onto his back before giving a toothless grin. Danny picked him up. 'What are we going to do now?'

The commotion woke Lulu up, and she started to cry. Chad picked her up. 'Let's settle them in the main bedroom, then we can bring them back in.'

Lulu and Louis had other ideas. It was refreshing to spend time with their uncles. They jumped up and down on their laps and giggled and smiled until Chad and Danny's arms ached. They put the twins down on the floor, and Chad built another tower of bricks. Lulu and Louis rocked backwards and forwards on their knees before starting their race. Lulu was in the lead until Louis overtook her to knock the bricks over. Danny clapped. 'My one won!'

Chad picked Lulu up. 'You *do* realise what's just happened, don't you?' Danny shook his head as he danced around the room, high-fiving Louis. 'They've started crawling. Millie and Jordan will be so disappointed to have missed that.'

Danny winked. 'Let's not tell them. We'll put the babies to bed now they've worn themselves out and keep their achievement a secret.'

*

By the end of the holiday, Millie and Jordan felt refreshed. They'd had lots of help this week and time to themselves. Millie was determined, though, to show Wilhelmina her house. She'd taken some photographs and took them out of her bag when she met Wilhelmina for coffee. 'So, there you go, these are for you. You can see where Wilfred's paintings of me have ended up and the one that Chad did.'

Wilhelmina scrutinised the photographs. 'Your home is so lovely, dear. I have only one suggestion to make.'

Millie sighed. Trust Wilhelmina to have the last say on something. 'What's that?'

'You should erect a swing in the branches of the

oak tree. Given the size of it, you could probably fit two.'

Millie nodded; she was relieved that was all Wilhelmina wanted to change. 'That sounds like a plan; I'll get Jordan onto it.'

*

Wilhelmina was sorry to see the young family leave at the end of their holiday; she went to her room to reflect. She sat at her dressing table and moved the miniature painting of her mother's engagement ring into the centre. She then reached into her handbag and displayed the photographs of Millie and Jordan's house around it.

Wilhelmina held a hand to her chest; she'd felt a connection to Jordan, and now she knew why – he'd bought her childhood home. Wilhelmina had lived in the Victorian house as a young girl. A scar on the oak tree brought back memories. Wilhelmina had been on her swing when a branch became loose, and her father had thrown the swing away. The tree was much older and stronger now, and Lulu and Louis would have fun on a swing each; Wilhelmina was sure of that.

It had been a sad day when Wilhelmina's parents said they could no longer afford the upkeep of the three-storey house in London and were moving to Devon. From Millie's account of the renovation work they'd undertaken; it appeared the house had been unloved for many years. Wilhelmina was delighted it was once again a happy home.

Wilfred emerged from his adjoining bedroom. 'I thought you might enjoy a romantic dinner for two tonight, so I've arranged for a table in the bar. Brett has agreed to play the piano.'

Wilhelmina raised her eyes. 'It's about time Brett did something.'

Wilfred frowned. 'Now, now. We love all of our grandsons in equal measure.'

*

Two prawn cocktails, half a lager, and a glass of sherry arrived before Wilfred reached across the table to hand his wife an envelope. He smiled. 'Go on, open it.'

Wilhelmina frowned as she tore open the envelope and read the card inside:

WELCOME TO HOLLYWOOD

Arrival: Late September

Departure: Early December

Address: Sunset Boulevard, Hollywood, USA

Terms & Conditions: Your job as Matriarch of the Harbottle family will be kept open for you during your autumn sabbatical.

Wilhelmina gulped. 'America! Why would I want to go there?!'

'Because you need to support your husband. I'm off to Hollywood.'

'Oh, for goodness sake.'

'I'm not joking. My whimsical paintings have taken off.'

Wilhelmina downed her sherry in one and ordered another. 'Will we go on any red carpets?'

Wilfred winked. 'Oh, I'm sure there'll be a red carpet or two. Will you join me on an adventure of a lifetime?'

Wilhelmina couldn't remember the last time she'd felt so excited. She took a deep breath before responding with a twinkle in her eye, 'Yes, dear, if I must.'

****

Printed in Great Britain
by Amazon

19670322R00144